GOLD

GOLD

KEEPER OF TIME

Jesse Lesniowski

To order additional copies of this book, contact:
Xlibris Corporation
1-888-795-4274
www.Xlibris.com
Orders@Xlibris.com
58660

Contents

Prologue

The unknown creature opened its eyes for the first time.

"Hello, little one," a sweet voice called to him.

He guessed that it must be his mother.

"He-llo," he replied, having trouble talking.

The blurred creature came closer to him. "Gold. That's what I'll name you." Her voice was sweetened with gladness.

With a smile, he went back to sleep under the fur of his mother.

Chapter 1

Separation

"Scatter!"

He heard someone shout out. He quickly locked eyes with his mother. He ran up to his mother and climbed onto her back, her golden red fur against his.

"Grab on and hold on tight! Don't let go!"

His vision was blurred as he and his mother jumped and ran through the trees, their tails dangling. He heard a sharp scream of a familiar group member, and then it faded away into the distance. As he went through the trees, bugs and bits of fruit pieces fell on his face, but he didn't notice. His mother stopped.

"Don't move," she whispered as she stood still.

Gold shifted his head to see what the fuss was about and saw a catlike creature staring at them from a thick branch—the same branch that they were on! He tried not to think of the vicious creature, but he couldn't get it out of his mind. The creature sniffed and looked in Gold's direction. The cold glare in its eyes made him flinch. The individual must have seen him twitch because it was walking toward him and his mother.

"I have the other newborn. Just run!" a voice called from above the next branch. With that, his mother bounded across the branch and over the cat. She followed the other tamarin, which Gold guessed was his father, and in his arm, his sibling. As his mother jumped, her long tail was caught by the cat's huge paw, its claws extended. His mother yowled in pain as blood squirted from the tip of her tail. He and his mother were pulled down from the branch.

"Gold! Just run! You can go on without me. Go find your father! His name is Jigsaw!"

He jumped off his mother as she struggled against the horrifying creature. "But . . . what is your . . . name, Mom?"

She looked at her son, tears coming. "Blume. Now run!"

Gold ran as fast as he could, his eyes flinching at every piece of air they took in. *Mom, please be okay.* He looked from side to side to find out where his father went. A chill went through him as he felt breath on the back of his fur. He slightly turned his head and saw a fairly big bird with a black beak, black feathers, and a massive wingspan. Without warning, the bird lifted off its feet, picked Gold up, and carried him away into the distant rain forest sky.

Gold woke up in a nest the next morning after his capture by the massive bird. He looked around the strawlike surrounding. It looked like a big bowl. In the middle of the bowl, there were three large eggs. They all sparkled as the sun rose from the trees. Monkey and other animal sounds roared up from the tree canopies. It took him a while to find out where he was. A crackling sound came from his left side. His head shifted as he saw a piece of liquid shell land in front of him. He turned his head to the direction it came from, the direction of the eggs. A black beak poked out from one of the eggs. The sharp beak pierced through the egg like it was a leaf. Then, Gold suddenly knew what he was here for—to be eaten!

The two-legged bird ran toward Gold. Its beak lunged for his stomach. This bird was larger than him. How was he, a newborn tamarin, supposed to run from this thing? Gold jumped to the top of the nest. The predator's beak got tangled at the side of the nest while Gold jumped to the other side. He noticed that the other eggs were hatching. He had to act fast if he wanted to keep his life. He looked behind him and noticed a branch about two paws' length away. He jumped for it. His tail in midair, he landed on the branch. He looked around. He wasn't home, not with his mother, not safe. His back gnawed with pain from the bird's talons. With his size, he was lucky he hadn't been killed then and there. He blinked and then climbed a vine to a high tree. He was safe there. Heat stroked through his fur, making him hungry. The figs on the top branch ahead of him made his stomach growl. He eventually ate the figs, one by one. The taste reminded him of home, possibly someplace he would never see again.

He thought back to that scary cat creature that had nearly killed him. The creature's eyes made him angry. Why should he be alone in the rain forest? It wasn't fair. As he looked below him, he saw many animals all walking together. He jumped higher. Not wanting to be seen, he jumped until he got to a ridged branch on top of the canopy. He couldn't spot his old tree. He knew what he had to do. Get home.

Chapter 2

Heraex

Gold looked at the sun. His eyes were closing, but he quickly opened them again. He didn't want to fall asleep. He didn't trust the world this time. Gold walked along a long, narrow branch.

"Why was it me—"

The crackling of a branch cut him off. The crackling sound grew louder, and he noticed it was beneath him. Running, he tried to get to the tree and to safety. It was too late. Soon he was free-falling down the rain forest canopy. Scratches and cuts bled as he scraped his skin against sticks and branches. A squeal of surprise shot out from his mouth when suddenly he felt a tug at his fur. He wasn't falling anymore; at least that was good. He looked up and saw another tamarin with a black body and a golden head and tail.

"T-thank you."

The other primate let out a groan of support, considering it couldn't open its mouth or he would fall. Thinking fast, Gold wrapped his tail around a nearby branch and pulled himself upward beside the other tamarin. The image was clearer now; she was female and looked no more than a few days older than him.

"You're welcome." There was amusement in her voice. "You're lucky I was here when I was or you would have been lunch for many predators down there, if you would've survived the fall."

She continued. "I haven't seen your kind around here in a while. You guys usually stay on the northern side of the rain forest. Either way, you're welcome to stay here."

Trying to catch his breath, Gold spoke, "Thank you. Who are you?" He tried not to sound rude.

"My name's Heraex. I'm a newborn here in the southeastern part. There is one thing I don't understand though. How did you get here?"

Gold told Heraex the whole story about the black bird and the cat creature, his head down.

"The ocelot! Did it follow you here?"

The concern in her eyes made Gold feel guilty for some odd reason. "No, well, at least I don't think so. I was carried away by a bird, remember?"

Heraex just turned her head and started walking toward the tree trunk. "Come, quickly!"

Gold staggered along the branch and into a slim gap in the tree trunk. He looked around and saw many other tamarins just like Heraex. He guessed it was her colony. It was much bigger than his. The trunk was filled with many perches and other gaps at different levels.

Gold peered out of a passing hole and saw clouds, dark ones. It would rain soon, and he would be stuck here. He continued following Heraex down the tree trunk.

"Just a bit farther," she hardly looked back when she said it. Vines and other plants were growing here in the tree, a perfect shelter from predators and the rain. He saw Heraex slip through a passageway. In the tunnel, it was cold and surprisingly light. Filtered holes in the bark made sunrays a common sight. The small tunnel suddenly turned to a big opening with no one in it. Heraex looked to one corner of the clearing and ran to it.

"What's going on?" asked Gold. When he got closer, he noticed another tamarin sleeping in the corner where Heraex ran.

"This is my mother. She somehow got bitten by an ocelot and has slept ever since." She directed at Gold.

Surely she doesn't think her mother is still alive? A bite from that monster woulda killed any tamarin. "How did she get here?" Gold asked.

"I brought her down here a while ago," she stuttered at her words.

He nodded and went closer to the body. Sure enough, she was breathing. Gold stared in awe. Pounding suddenly began all around them.

Gold ducked down. "What is that?" The pounding still roared in his ears; it was coming from all around him.

"Don't worry, it's just rain."

Gold felt cold at his feet. He looked down and spotted water. He remembered the holes in the bark. The place was going to flood!

"We have to get out of here. It's going to flood."

Heraex didn't even turn her head. "I know."

This reply startled him. Without another word, Gold darted off to where he came in to the tree trunk.

Chapter 3

Rainstorm

Gold hastily climbed up the tree trunk. He looked around and saw many more of the tamarins hiding behind the bark or behind a leaf. They looked at him in amazement. Without noticing them, he kept climbing. He didn't want to be in this tree anymore. The earlier remark from Heraex really scared him, and now he wouldn't stop at anything. His golden fur bounced every time he sprang from perch to perch. He looked down from a perch he was resting on. He heard a crash. The tree trunk was flooding with water!

Gold was only in the middle of the trunk and had no hope of getting out in time; the water was coming up fast, to make things worse. Water lapped at his feet as he struggled to get to higher ground. With his fur drenched, he probably wouldn't be able to climb very far up. The water climbed higher until he was surrounded by it entirely. Struggling for air, he rose up to the surface, but the current tugged him down again. The water was choking him, and he knew he hadn't much time to live.

All the other tamarins were still watching from their perches, as if they knew it would happen. They all watched him motionlessly. Crashing waves woke him from his trance, and he realized he was on a dry perch just above the water. The water was still rising, but he was safe on his perch for now. Gold looked to his side; it was Heraex! She had saved him from dying.

"Thank you, Heraex," he said with no tone.

She just gave him a look and started climbing. Her blinking blue eyes told him that he had to follow. The water was still rising, and he hadn't much time to get to the top. He kept wondering why Heraex was so nonchalant about the tragic event that was about to occur. Finally, they were out on a branch, sheltered from the rain and with the protection of the canopy.

When enough energy was gathered, Gold stood up and walked along the branch.

"Where are you going?" Heraex asked.

"Away from here! This place has death surrounding it! And what about your mother? Is she down in the tree drowning?" He let out a sigh. He had never experienced this kind of anger before.

Heraex just looked up at the sky. She opened her mouth and then closed it again. Finally, she got it out. "Well, to put it this way, she's stuck, and so is everyone else in that tree."

Gold couldn't figure out if she was crying or if rain had spattered her eyes. It took a while for Gold to get out of his paralyzed state. "What do you mean? Stuck?"

Heraex kept looking up as if she wanted to be somewhere up there. "We are stuck in . . . time."

A whirl of surprise swept through him. If she was stuck in time, how could she be here now?

"I know what you're thinking. We could never die. We are immune to death for about one million years now," she replied.

That's why she is an extraordinary color! She was here a million years ago! Her species is extinct. Come to think of it, all those tamarins in the tree are from a long time ago too. "What about your mother?"

Heraex looked straight at him. The thunder in the sky matched her voice. "She is literally frozen in time. No one really knows how it happened, but it had something to do with an ocelot, the same one from a million years ago."

Her drenched fur stuck to her body as she ran beside him. Come to think of it, she had abilities beyond Gold's imagination. Her feet were smaller, and her tail was longer than his own. And her hips looked like they could jump fifty feet across the rain forest.

She rubbed up to him. "I'll help you find your mother. I'll help you find your colony, and better yet, I'll guide you. I know this place better than anyone. I need a little excitement in my life."

Excitement? She's stuck in time! If that isn't enough excitement I would grow feathers. Gold thought. "The rain is pretty bad. Shouldn't we wait here until it's over?" It was getting dark too. He really needed to rest after learning all of this.

Heraex shook her head and lied down on the thick branch they were standing on. Gold did the same and quickly, with the sound of soothing raindrops, drifted into dreamland.

The clouds were white, and Gold was standing in a tree he had never seen before. It was dark green and very crooked. The trees were extremely far apart too. It would be impossible to jump that far without cracking your head open on the forest floor and some carnivore eating you. He heard some rustling in the bushes.

"You'll never catch me!"

To Gold's surprise, a tamarin a lot like Heraex's species came onto the branch he was resting on. The primate ran, not noticing Gold. They would collide! He closed his eyes and waited for the impact, but after a few seconds, there was none. The monkey had passed through him! Was he a ghost?

"Yah, I will!" Another monkey bounded onto the branch.

Oh, figs, it was Heraex! Her body stretched as she jumped across to the other tree about twenty feet away. Gold couldn't believe what he just saw. He was in Heraex's time, before she got stuck. Gold heard a snarl from the direction that Heraex and the other monkey went to. It sounded different, but it was a lot like an ocelot! He bounded across the closest branches and saw the ocelot confronting Heraex and the other primate.

The creature did not look like a present-day ocelot. It had a more muscular build and sharper fangs, and it was white and gray. It had no comparison whatsoever to the one that attacked him. Without warning, the ocelot jumped on the other tamarin. Blood spattered from the monkey's neck onto a nearby tree trunk.

"No, Baulex!" Tears streamed down Heraex's face as the horrific creature ripped Baulex's arm off and devoured it whole. More blood splattered on the trunk of the tree. Something was familiar about this place. But it wasn't his time zone. He had to leave!

He watched helplessly as the rest of the primate was devoured. The beast was so horrendous that it even walked up to the tree and licked the blood off the bark. The tree then seemed to give off a glow. The picture began to fade, getting darker and darker by the second.

"Mom, no!" The scream came from out of the darkness. There were a few snarls, and then it was over, blackness shrouded Gold.

Gold woke up with a surge of surprise. *It was just a dream.* He thought to himself. At least he hoped it was. Gold looked to his side; Heraex was gone. This time, Gold wasn't surprised. He simply got up and started walking through the thick branches of the rain forest canopy. Why did this happen to him? He was separated from his mother; he never met his sibling or his father, Jigsaw; and now these weird dreams? The only person he had now was Heraex, but of course, she was a million years old. Thunder still roared in his ears, and the rain still did not stop coming down. When would the rain end? *So many questions. I just wish I could answer them all.* He thought to himself.

"I'm over here, Gold."

He looked up to find his friend munching on some figs and oranges. He climbed up a narrow branch and joined Heraex.

"Why haven't you asked questions about how we came to be s-stuck?" she stuttered on the word.

Should I tell about my dream? No, I'll keep it a secret just for now. "Uh, I have a lot on my mind lately." He lied.

Heraex gave him a compassionate nod and kept on eating the fruits. "Anyway, it's still raining. Very odd, considering it's been thirteen hours now," said Heraex.

It actually was very odd. Gold's damp fur quivered at the thought of something supernatural. Was it? Or was it just the weather?

"Heraex!" an unidentified voice called out from the tree that they had escaped from.

Isn't the tree flooded?

"Coming!" Heraex called back, then turning to Gold, "You might want to stay . . ."

He followed Heraex to the entrance of the tree. He watched as she jumped through the water like it was air. Could she possibly be immune to the effects of being in water?

After a few moments had passed, Heraex returned. "Okay, let's go."

Puzzled, Gold looked at her, but without question, he followed her down the tree branches and on to other ones in the pursuit of looking for his family. A loud burst of thunder shot through his ears as he ran. Light enclosed on his eyes as a flash of lightning flared. This was indeed a major rainstorm.

Without warning, another flash of light streaked down the sky. It felt warmer on this tree. In fact, it was burning hot. This tree was on fire! It must have been the lightning that flared a few seconds ago.

"Gold! I could go through the fire, but you can't. How will you get around?"

He didn't know what to say. The fire was getting closer. The only thing that he could do was jump to the forest floor. "I'll jump!" he screamed out.

"Are you crazy? You'll get killed from the impact."

Gold ignored her and jumped out of the tree. Raindrops still poured on him, making it seem like he was underwater. He looked up while he fell, but it was impossible to see from the blinding raindrops. He still saw the light from the burning tree, but it began to fade as he fell. As he hit the floor, it wasn't that much of an impact. It seemed like a splash. And yet, it was! He landed in a rain forest river! He quickly sank to the bottom as he had not the energy to rise back up. Enclosed in water again, he was slowly losing consciousness and drifted away into the river.

Chapter 4

River Beasts

Gold woke up to a clicking sound. He didn't care though; he was alive, and that was all that mattered. The clicking sound was still in the air. Even though it was still raining, he could feel air against his fur.

Opening his eyes, he realized he was moving. He looked around and saw a huge waterfall with vines on rocks and trees with huge ferns. There was still water all around him. Maybe Heraex had come to rescue him again. He looked down. "Thank you, He—" His voice trailed off. This wasn't Heraex. It was a fish—a big pink one too. He had never seen anything like it before. Beside him, there swam another one, not quite as pink, but pink enough. He let out a huge gasp.

This must have caught the river beast's attention. Clicks came from its mouth as it spoke, "Ah, I see you're up! Yay! I'm so excited I met a new friend!" Its playful voice surprised Gold. He didn't expect this beast to be so chipper, a little too chipper at that.

"Is he awake?" the other creature asked. The river beast he was riding on made a playful nod and did a playful flip in the water. These creatures were very sloth-headed, considering that when the beast did a flip, he was put underwater. When it finished its weird little flip, Gold out came gasping for air.

"Oh, sorry. Did I accidentally drown you?"

Gold was filled with anger. *You think? You overgrown fish!* he thought angrily. "Oh, I'm fine," he said, trying to hide his anger. These things saved his life; the least he could do was give a little respect even though it was hard. "Thank you for saving me." These words were becoming very familiar to him. He seemed to always have to get saved from something.

"It's okay. At least I have a new friend!"

Gold just rolled his eyes and lay back down on its back. Once in a while, he felt a twitch on the river beast's back, as if it was restraining itself from flipping again. He felt relief once the creatures got to a nearby rock. He quickly let out a jump and rested on a rock. The two creatures just stared at him with four beady eyes, as if they wanted to play. Gold was uncomfortable from the idea of always being watched by these things. Their heads looked very disoriented, and their snouts were very long and pink. He had never seen a weird-looking creature like this before. They both let out clicks that lasted about a second each, but kept their eyes on him. Gold shifted to the other side of the rock. Would they eat him? This was the thought that surrounded him. Almost everything he had run into wanted to eat him.

"What are you?" the beast on the left said.

What am I? I should be asking you. "Well, I'm what they call a tamarin. A golden lion tamarin, to be exact.

"How did you get here?" the one on the right asked.

Gold wasn't sure if he should tell them his story. These were strange creatures that hadn't earned his trust yet. "I came from a tree," he said, trying to be polite and give them as little information as he possibly could. The beasts looked at each other and did a happy flip in the air. The show was beautiful, but weird at the same time.

"Well, what are you?" Gold finally got out.

While still doing flips the beasts said, "We are *Inia geoffrensis.*" Gold wanted to knock some sense into these things. "That is our scientific name. We are not going to tell you our species name or our real names." They each gave out these crooked smiles.

Gold was scared now. Now he was sure that they would probably eat him. Gold spotted a splash of water out of his right eye. He could then see one of the beasts swimming up to it very fast. It quickly opened its jaws and snatched the creature. Blood swiveled out of its body as the beast brought it to the other beast. It was a fish that it had killed. A foul stench came from it as they ripped it opened and swallowed it whole. Gold thought he might vomit. Where was Heraex? He needed her now.

These creatures looked like they were flawed in design. Now that he noticed, these beasts were huge! They looked as if they were sixteen tamarins long.

"Okay, I think that we should keep going," one beast said. The other one nodded, and both looked at Gold. "Are you coming?"

What a stupid question! Of course I'm coming. Do they really expect me to stay on this rock until someone helps me? He ignored their question and jumped on the back of one beast. "Where are we going?" he asked patiently, waiting for a stupid answer. He didn't even know why he asked.

"We are going to the north side to breed." They seemed like they wanted to have a child. But it was perfect! He needed to go to the north side to find his colony. He could use these whatever-they-were to find his mom! So he went onto the back of the creature he hardly knew.

It had been a few hours since Gold had gotten off the rock. The beast's back began to get bumpy and ridged after a while. The rain was still pouring down, but that wasn't the only reason he was wet. The beast kept flipping in the water, forgetting that he was on its back. Gold was very annoyed with the river beasts. He couldn't believe how a creature so big could be so stupid. It maddened him so much that he could sink his claws into its rubbery skin right now. Either way, they were going to the north, and that was all that mattered to him.

"Oh, no!"

This sound woke Gold out of his trancelike state. He looked around but saw nothing.

"What's wrong?" the other one questioned.

"I can sense piranhas with my echolocation!"

Echolocation? What was that? Gold heard little clicks from the beasts. Was that echolocation? He had no time to think though. He did know what piranhas were. His mom had told him stories about them.

One day there was a golden tamarin that decided to go in a rain forest river. After he went in, he never came up . . . alive that is. His bones shot up from the bottom of the lake without flesh, fur, or skin. The horrific fish stripped the tamarin clean from life.

And he was about to be the same if he didn't think of something now. "Are you sure? If there are, we should go in the opposite direction. There is no fighting piranhas."

They both nodded and turned. Gold was speechless, how could these creatures live in water? It was way too dangerous. A loud screech came from the creature beside him. A streak of blood came out of the beast as it swam awkwardly.

"Piranhas!" the beast screamed. "Leave. I'll catch up!"

The beast that Gold was on made a sharp turn. He struggled to stay on. If he fell in the water, there was no coming back. He dared not look back at the other river beast. Rain spattered his face as he held on tight. The beast was going so fast that it felt like they were flying. He finally decided to look back and saw a lifeless body floating in the distance. The other river beast was dead! It was hard to believe that those little fishes could kill a nine-foot river beast. A few tamarin lengths away, Gold saw fishes hopping, and their jaws snapping open and close.

"Hurry! They are catching up!" Without warning, the river beast sped up at a tremendous speed. There was no stopping now. A clap of thunder crashed in his ears, then another. *Wait, thunder can't crash two times in a row.* This was weird. Then the idea suddenly came to him.

"Stop! We're going to go over a waterfall!" His scream could be heard from a mile away. A shock of death went through Gold as the river beast sharply stopped. Its tail flipped to the air, and the rest of its body followed as it flew through the air. But it couldn't stop in time. Mist from the waterfall shrouded Gold and the beast. They made a huge splash as they entered the water again. The crashing of the water roared in Gold's ears as they fell down and down once again into the quick rapids of the water below.

Chapter 5

Through the Eyes of Heraex

Heraex sat on a tree drenched from the rain. She couldn't believe how long this rainstorm lasted. But the sound of the crashing waterfall next to her seemed to soothe her.

"That tamarin has something he isn't telling me. I just know it," she thought out loud. But what was he hiding? She would probably never find out, considering he was lost, maybe even dead. What really puzzled her was that he landed in water. She just looked at the beautiful waterfall. *After all these years, this waterfall is still here.* The thought swiveled around her like a snake. She suddenly heard a sharp, screaming chirp from the distance of the waterfall. "Gold!" she said to herself and ran to the waterfall.

Leaves smacked her face as she ran to the roar of the waterfall. It was right in front of her the whole time. If Gold had fallen in the river, it wouldn't take that much time for him to get carried away to the waterfall. Heraex quickly climbed up to the top of the tree she had just landed on. Through a gap in the leaves, she saw the waterfall, her black hair mixing with the canopy. A small gold blotch continued to fall down the waterfall the way she saw it, and another massive pink creature followed him down. After she saw this, she kept on jumping through the canopy, hoping she would get there in time. She didn't know if the pink creature was a friend or a foe. *I must get there before it is too late.* Jumping out of the last tree to the river, the rain still fell on her head. She finally got to the forest floor. The forest floor was very dangerous for some animals might eat you.

She finally came to the beginning of the river. A sudden bump in the water appeared and was heading straight for Heraex! As it finally got out of the water, it revealed itself. It had a scaly body that was speckled with

He looked back and saw his golden fur floating down to the forest floor. Once again, the images were begging to fade away. He became shrouded in darkness and found himself awake underneath Heraex's head.

"Gold, you were talking in your sleep. Did you have a bad dream?"

Gold wondered if he should tell. Well, of course he should. She was in the dream. But first he asked, "How did you get stuck in time in the first place?"

Heraex took her hands from shaking Gold awake and told him the story. She was wondering why Gold went straight into this conversation. "Well, I was playing catch-up with my other newborn friend, and we ran into this ocelot."

This was rapidly making sense to him. All the things that he experienced in his dream were coming true.

Heraex continued, "He killed my friend and devoured him whole, bones and fur. After that, he decided to come after me. My mother tried to save me but ended up getting bitten by the prehistoric ocelot. Then, this glow came from the tree. It spread through all of us, the other things in the tree, the tree itself, and other primates, even insects that were in the tree at the time. After that, I really don't know what happened. The ocelot tried to attack me, but I healed myself, and then I heard something, something like a scared shriek. I looked over and saw a yellow blur in the trees. It soon disappeared, but I also found this golden material. I didn't know what it was, so I easily discarded it."

Gold was paralyzed. He couldn't believe what he had just heard. If he was part of the past, then wasn't he part of the present? Maybe he traveled through time. He didn't know. How could all of this happen in one night when it happened over a million years ago?

"And the ocelot is still stalking through this rain forest, ready to kill at any moment." Heraex concluded.

He remembered now! His mother also used to tell him stories about the prehistoric ocelot, about how it once killed one of his relatives down the line. *Emprolla*, I think it was. But how he was remembering all of this just at this moment was all together strange. When his second dream had occurred just a few hours ago, it felt so real. Yet it was a million years ago! He still knew that he and Heraex had to keep going if they want to find his mother and all the rest of his group. He would be so happy, finally meeting up with his parents.

"Heraex, we should start going now. We can't keep waiting for this storm to blow over because we both know it's not going to happen anytime soon." Gold still was amazed by how long this storm had lasted. Some usually lasted a few hours, but this was a mark in history. Without another thought, the two tamarins got up and shot into the drenched trees.

Chapter 7

The Tree of Gold

"So it's made out of gold, you say?"

Gold nodded as he swung through the branches of the rain forest canopy. He was telling Heraex the story about the tree of gold, one of his favorite stories that his mom used to tell him.

There was once a tree that had bark that shined like gold in the morning sun. Many wanted some of the bark for themselves, but once they took it, unfortunate things started happening to them. This one tamarin took a piece of bark and died from the bite of a boa. The next time someone took a piece, they got caught in a snare. No one has ever taken a piece from the tree ever again. Nobody even lives in it. Other animals say that no one lives in it because no one is worthy of its shelter.

Rain still poured down on Heraex's face as he told her this. She was clearly interested in his stories, but he was also curious about hers. There was no time to ask though. He needed to get shelter from this rain soon, or he would literally drown in thin air. As he looked up and down for shelter, Heraex went off to get some dinner. It had now been two days since he had had the second dream. It still haunted him to know he could travel through time. Tonight he wouldn't sleep; they needed the extra guard anyway. The world had proven itself to be a wicked and wretched forest.

"Mango or oranges?" Heraex questioned.

"Oranges," he replied, grabbed one, and started eating it. He would certainly pick oranges over any fruit. They simply tasted better, and they were juicier too.

"What if the tree is real?" Heraex asked, almost seeming to jump out of her fur from excitement. If he gave her an answer, either way it would turn out bad.

"I think so. What good is a story if it isn't real?" he said, regretting his answer.

Heraex smiled and continued eating her mango. "Could we look for it?" she asked in between mouthfuls.

"A tree of gold, you say? That would be perfect for my collection. If I shall rule the world of the forest of rain, I should have gold." The sly voice came out from a shadowy bush. He had been watching Heraex and this new tamarin for days. If he couldn't kill Heraex, he'd kill the golden monkey.

"It's settled. I'll follow them to it and take some gold. Nothing will happen to me. I'm immune to death anyway," the prehistoric animal said. Although his fur was drenched from the rain, this would not stop him. He was already king of the ocelots. All he had to do was become king of everything else. A deep purr of laughter came from his throat. Evil surrounded his eyes, and he busted out of the bush he was under and went under the tree where the two monkeys had rested for the night. He could taste tamarin blood now. His mouth opened, and his white pointy fangs were exposed. He began to salivate. This would be a good meal.

The next day, Gold opened his eyes. At least he didn't have a dream this time. Although he had tried to fight sleep, it was useless. Sleep was a natural part of life, and no one could fight life. Well, maybe Heraex. The sun was out, but the rain still poured. It had been a week and a half since this tragic storm happened. Come to think of it, it happened when Gold first went into the tree. *Must be a coincidence*, he thought to himself. Heraex was still asleep on the branch beside him. Her black fur looked like skin from the wetness on her body. Didn't she want to look for the tree?

"Heraex, I don't mean to wake you but—"

Heraex turned around, but she didn't look like Heraex at all. Its eyes were red, it had huge fangs, and it had Heraex in its mouth. It threw her off and pounced on Gold. He screamed in terror.

"Gold! Are you okay?" Gold saw Heraex's head right above him. "You were having a shadow dream."

Gold jumped to his feet and looked at Heraex. It was a dream, and Heraex was all right.

"Was that another time dream?" Gold shook his head. This had been the second time Heraex had woken him up, and it had begun to get very annoying. Gold looked around. It looked exactly as it did in his dream, and his thoughts seemed to linger in his mind.

"Could we please go and find the tree of gold?" Heraex asked.

This was hard to answer. He looked at Heraex's pleading eyes.

"Fine, but as soon as we are done, we have to go to the north," he reassured.

Heraex jumped in excitement and pulled on Gold's fur with her arm. They jumped through the rain together.

"What do you think it looks like?"

Gold really didn't know what to say. "Umm, gold," he got out.

Heraex gave a sarcastic cough and bounded through the trees.

"Gold? Do you know where it says it is in the story?"

Come to think of it, he did. "Yeah, between three green rocks in the middle of the forest."

They were nearly in the middle of the forest. Gold looked around and saw lots of green but not the rocks. Through all of the rain, Gold spotted something glowing in the distance.

"There it is. There it is!" Heraex said while jumping up and down.

They continued running through the branches and finally reached a clearing with ferns and grass, but no trees. It wasn't too much of a big clearing, but big enough. And sure enough, in the middle was a gold tree. Only the bark was gold though.

"Look, the green rocks are even surrounding it!" Heraex pointed out. Sure enough, she was right. It was such an amazing sight that not many animals could get to see.

"Move out of my way!"

Gold got pushed over into a tree and lay there on the forest floor. He looked up and saw an ocelot, but it was a different one. It must be the one from a million years ago. He looked over at Heraex; she was also pushed against a tree. He watched helplessly as the animal stripped many pieces of bark off the tree with its claws. He just had to tell the story! How stupid! Now a legend was being destroyed, and it was his entire fault. Gold heard footsteps coming up to him. It was that stupid ocelot.

"I'll come back for you later," it said between the pieces of golden bark coming from its mouth. The words seemed to stab at him. He was wanted dead!

"Gold, are you okay? That monster hit us pretty hard."

He could easily agree with her on that one. "I'm okay. Oh, figs! I just had to say that story out loud! How stupid of me!" He felt so much sadness. All of this was his fault, and he could do nothing to fix it. *Unless.* "I could go back in time to stop this from ever happening! I could stop myself from telling this story!"

Heraex looked at him with confusion. "I don't know. You could end up changing history." Wariness flashed in her eyes.

"It's a risk I'll have to take. I have to sleep now, so shush!"

Heraex let out a little humph and walked toward a tree to sleep on. Gold quickly followed and began to drift off into dreamland.

"Be careful." Those were the last words he heard.

"Where am I?" Gold wondered as he looked around. It had been two days since he had told the story; hopefully he was in the right time. All of the trees and plants looked the same, and it was raining too. It even looked like the same night. He managed to hear the words, "tree of gold" and "not worthy of its shelter." He knew that he was close. Maybe even closer than he expected. He had been transported to the top of the tree that they rested on that one night! Rain still poured down on the forest. He looked down at the two drenched tamarins. *Oh, no! I already started telling the story!* Without another word, he swung down from the top of the tree. "STOP!" It was too late. The past Gold had already finished telling the story.

"Who are you?" Heraex turned around and asked.

No! I can't change history too much, he thought. So he bounded off through the trees and suddenly found himself glowing. "Here we go again!" he shouted as he disappeared from that time period.

He appeared in daylight as he saw a monstrous animal pushed two monkeys aside. *That must be us!* He never knew how far he had gotten pushed, but now he knew, and it was horrifying to even think of. He saw the ocelot came up to his past self and said those terrifying words: "I'll come back for you later." They still lingered in his mind. He hid in a bush as the creature darted past him and ran into the distance. He got what he came here for, and Gold wasn't able to stop him.

"Who are you?" he heard himself call. He tried to run, but Heraex caught up with him with her powerful legs.

"Are you here to steal the bark too? I should knoc—Gold?"

The past Gold came to Heraex. "Yeah?" He looked at the future Gold in astonishment. "Me?" the past Gold said, amazed.

He tried to hide his face. "Yes, but I only came here to stop that thing."

Heraex looked at the past Gold. "What do you mean?"

He quickly told them the story about what had just happened and how he came into the past to stop himself from telling the story. The past Gold nodded approvingly and put out his hand to help him up.

"Here, I'll help you."

Gold looked up at his mirror self. "NO!" After that, the two Golds starting glowing, and within a flash they were gone. Gold woke up with the other Gold by his side. Oh, was this ever a bad idea!

Chapter 8

Himself

"So let me get this straight. You brought yourself from the past?" Heraex seemed to glow with anger. "Don't you know how dangerous this is?"

The past Gold spoke up, "Same old Heraex."

Heraex looked over at him. "Was I talking to you?" she said sarcastically.

"Well, actually, yeah."

Her eyes were locked on the past Gold. "Put a fig in it!"

Gold had never seen Heraex act this way before, so full of anger, especially at him. He was full of astonishment. She turned back toward him.

"You do know that there is no way of getting this . . . you back."

Gold never really thought of that before. He didn't even mean to bring himself here. How would he get himself back, and what about the past Heraex?

"She'll do fine," the past Gold stated.

Gold looked amazingly at the past one. *How did he know what I was thinking?*

Well, I'm you, so I guess we can share thoughts.

But how can you hear me in my head?

I don't really know yet.

The fact that he was having a conversation with himself bothered Gold. How could this be? How could anything be in the weird forest? *First, there was me meeting a million-year-old monkey, then I could travel through time. All of these bizarre enemies and now this? How could I live with myself? Or . . . himself.*

"Why are both of you so quiet?" Heraex questioned them demandingly.

Should we tell her? asked past Gold.

Of course. She's our best friend.

Okay, I'll tell her.

After that conversation, the past Gold cleared his throat. "Gold and I are the same person, right?"

Heraex nodded while past Gold continued. "So we can talk to each other in our heads."

Heraex didn't seem too shocked when she heard this. "You guys have what is called mind chat. It's when you can communicate telepathically."

This is so cool! But how are they supposed to get the past Gold back to his own time?

Yeah, how will I get back to my own time period? Heraex must be worried sick about me right now.

I'm not sure yet. Maybe if I dream again, you could somehow come back with me. I have no control of when I dream or how I dream.

Suddenly, an idea just took over him. If the past Gold was just from a few days ago, he could travel through time too! Without any further ado, he addressed this to Heraex.

"It's never going to work."

Why did she have to be so negative all the time about it?

"Since you're the regular Gold in this time, you might be the only one that has that ability. The world was only meant for one Gold to be in this time period, and only one Gold could have the power."

This made sense to him, but now there was no hope in getting himself back.

"Let's eat," Heraex said with a tint of anger in her voice. The two Golds followed her to an orange tree.

It's still raining in your time? past Gold asked.

Yeah, it's very strange.

If it doesn't stop soon, there will be massive floods.

I know. It has been going on for two and a half weeks so far.

Gold decided to take one of the biggest oranges from the tree canopy. The past Gold probably did the same thing because they are the same tamarin. Gold pierced a claw through the peel of the orange. He quickly stuck it in his mouth and started to eat the insides. Oranges were the most important food for him. He loved them!

"Be careful, okay?" warned Heraex.

Is she talking to us? present Gold asked.

"For what?"

Heraex glanced at the two Golds. "If the present Gold gets hurt, it simply won't matter, but if the past Gold gets hurt, that will affect the present one. Same with death."

Shocked, Gold looked at himself. *Okay, we have to be extra careful now.*

I agree. I don't want to die if you do. Gold wondered if he said that in a rude way.

I know what your thinking, and don't worry. I am you, remember?

Yeah, I guess, but this is all so strange.

Tell me about it.

"Okay, if you guys are going to have a little conversation with yourselves, then say it out loud! I don't want to be left out."

Why is Heraex so angry about this stuff? It doesn't concern her.

I agree.

Get out of my head!

The past Gold put his head down in embarrassment. Gold felt sorry for what he said to himself, but he soon got over it.

"So the ocelot still stole the bark?" asked Heraex.

The past Gold looked at Heraex. "Yeah, unfortunately. What do you think he'll do with it?"

The present Gold was kind of sad that he wasn't in the conversation. He let it carry on.

"He might harvest the energy, or he might keep the gold to tell people that he is their king or something like that."

Gold couldn't believe what he was hearing. This was outrageous! He couldn't believe that an ocelot could cause all of this damage.

"I think that we should keep moving on, don't you both?"

The two Golds nodded and followed Heraex down the tree branches and down the vines. He had always enjoyed swinging off vines, but his mother had always told him to be careful or he might fall. Even though he was still young, he was very brave. Even Heraex thought so too.

"So we've been searching for the north for six hours, and now you tell me you don't know where it is?" Her eyes flashed in anger once again. "Well, if you put it that way." Heraex just turned her head and lay down on a branch. "I'm going to sleep, and I don't care if you two sleep or not."

Okay, well, she didn't have to be so snobby about it.

She's usually like this when she gets mad.

Well, I think that I might go to sleep too. I'm really tired.

All right. Good night . . . me.

Gold decided to go to sleep too. He lay down on the branch next to the past Gold. He looked at himself. It was like looking in a mirror. He was looking at himself.

Chapter 9

Howlers

Gold couldn't sleep at all that night. He kept thinking of all of the things that had happened to him over the past few weeks. He heard moans from the past Gold. This meant he was probably waking up. He looked at him.

What are you doing up so early? past Gold asked.

I couldn't sleep. I was thinking.

Really? I never used to stay up all night and think.

Well, I've changed! All of us have!

Okay, well, you don't have to get all mad.

Gold looked away from his gaze. Rain was still pouring down. Would he ever get a break from all of this? He looked at the river in the distance. It was higher than when he had last seen it. If this rain didn't stop soon, it would cause a lot of serious trouble to lots of animals in the forest of rain.

"Hey, Gold?" It was Heraex.

"Why are you up?" Gold heard a deep growl coming from Heraex's stomach.

"I'm hungry, as you can see."

Gold let out a chirp of laughter. At least she was in a better mood today. "There is no fruit on this tree. We should move on to find some more food. Actually, I haven't seen food in a while over here."

Heraex seemed to agree with him. He made a quick glance behind him to see what the past Gold was up to. He was just sitting on a branch taking an air bath. Air baths are taking baths in midair. When it rains, some tamarins go out in the rain and groom themselves. It works out very well too.

"Okay, Golds! Let's move out to find some food." Both of them nodded and ran in front of Heraex. She swiftly caught up to them and led the way.

Why does she always have to lead the way?
Yeah, I don't get it either.

Gold was tremendously annoyed with this mind-chat ability. The other Gold was driving him figs! If this didn't stop soon, he'd make it stop. As the three tamarins stopped for a rest near a high tree, Gold watched the rain fall on leaves and then drip down to the forest floor. It was amazing how nature could be so beautiful but at the same time devastating.

He gently licked raindrops off leaves, as he usually did when he was thirsty. Rainwater was tremendously delicious, way better than river water. He had had enough of rivers for one lifetime. With each minute passing, he began to grow hungrier and hungrier. If he didn't find food soon, he would faint. And he thought the same with Heraex and the past Gold.

"Okay, I think we should move on again. We have had too much of a rest," said Heraex.

Gold agreed with her. Even though it was nice on this tree with the dark green leaves and the amber sunrise, he had to get going to find some food. He hadn't really gone that far from the tree of Gold. It would be no problem getting back. With that, he trailed off into the forest once again.

"Hey, I found something!" Gold said as he walked toward a leaf that looked like a heart. Sure enough, it was attached to a small tree. Heraex and past Gold walked up to him.

"Are there any fruits in it?" Heraex asked.

Gold pushed his way through the leaves; they seemed to brush against him. But there were no fruits in this tree. Heraex and past Gold decided to help Gold.

"Wow! This tree has hairs!" past Gold exclaimed.

The two Golds looked in bewilderment. It did have hairs. "I'm getting out of this tree. It's way too weird for me." As Gold walked out of the tree, he could feel itching on his skin. He sat down and started to groom himself as all tamarins do. He looked in a gap between the heart-shaped leaves. Heraex and past Gold jumped out of that very opening. He watched both of them; they seemed to be doing the same exact thing that he had been doing a few seconds ago. This was strange, but so was everything else in this forest.

"Are you itchy too?" Gold asked them both. They both nodded, vigorously trying to relieve their skins. Suddenly, a heat wave came over Gold. His head felt like it was burning. He was suddenly very weak and unable to move. It even looked like the others were doing the same. Gold quietly collapsed on the forest floor, vulnerable to predators. He had fainted.

"Eih hingyao wactikala wafikambala chikitama fotalala becogeta grinkolata."

Gold woke up to this strange chant. He was feeling better too. His fever was gone, and he could now move.

"Kia determa ka! Oasey lada tokalalada."

Where are these words coming from?

"Ditamarangtodfal oka do ka titimana, kitadoda KA!"

The chanting suddenly stopped as he turned his head and found these monkeys pointing at him. There were five, and they were very large. Compared to him, that is. One walked up to him. It was blonde with a black face that poked out of its hair. All of the other monkeys had black faces too, but they were all different colors. They each had very long tails that seemed to wrap around branches as they walked. They had claws that easily crunched through bark.

Another walked up to him; its color was black, with a hint of blonde at the stomach. Gold never thought monkeys of the same species could be of different colors. His species wasn't; they were just all gold colors. One with red fur walked up to Gold also. The other two stayed on the other side with past Gold and Heraex.

"You are monkey?" the blonde one said.

Gold nodded his head and blinked. He opened his eyes, but the primates were still there.

"We are monkey! We be allies!"

These primates were very bad at speaking. They obviously hadn't heard anyone but themselves in a long time.

"Where am I?" Gold asked. These were monkeys; they were a part of his species. They wouldn't hurt him. The black one moved up to him.

"We are in gold tree."

His eyes busted with alarm. No one was supposed to live in the tree of gold! Or maybe they were too scared with these monkeys living here. He had no facts to work with. Each of them let out a huge sounding howl.

"OHHH WHOOOOO!" they each whistled. It seemed to lighten up the whole forest.

He looked out of the corner of his eye and saw Heraex and past Gold standing up. They were probably wakened by the howls. He watched as the two other monkeys explained things to them. They both had a burnt red color but of different shades. They must be like the guards between these five monkeys; the thought of having guards scared him. *Why would they need two large monkeys for guards?*

The blonde one walked closer to him. "We are howlers. Monkeys of howl! We howl into the night and day, and we rule the middle of the forest of rain!"

Gold backed up. "So you must be very powerful," Gold stated.

"Yes, indeed, I am. I am the leader of the howlers."

Gold understood now. One thing he still didn't understand was how he had been healed from the fever. "How did I get healed, and how did we even get here?" Gold questioned.

"You have brushed yourselves against a stinging tree. When it comes in contact with skin, it usually makes you have an itching sensation. Then after that, you get fever. All of you seemed to have and passed out on the forest floor. I don't know how long you all have been there, but lucky for you that my howlers passed at the time they did."

Gold was very thankful. "Oh, thank you!" Gold said while he looked at his two other group members. They both watched him carefully. The black howler stepped in.

"No need for thanks. We must be getting to chanting. You can watch, but don't help us!"

Gold was taken aback by this remark. Heraex ran up to him and nuzzled him on the back. Past Gold came up too, but he kept his distance. The five howlers walked up to this weird-looking statue stuck in the golden tree behind most of its golden leaves.

All of them continued to dance around the statue and chant. "Hualrivds huaka didadadidoduadaaifme! Ufff somwaga tootajeh! Malalawakajajaja!"

The statue that they danced around seemed to look like another monkey. Gold came closer to the statue without the other monkeys noticing too much. His eyes zoomed in to read an inscription on the gold statue. It read, "God Mala-mala, encrapture toatoo defangyeax fieun de fanaslisee goeprapapa simtanuy Mala-mala huryeasf digees FALLA GOLD!" Gold looked in confusion. He obviously didn't know this language.

"Heraex? Do you know this kind of language?"

Heraex walked up to take a closer peek at the inscription. "I understand a little, but the rest is a blur to me. It says, 'God Mala-mala, creator of the forest of rain, shall return once again to find his . . . something Gold.' That's pretty much all I could make out."

Although he now understood a little bit, he still didn't understand the meaning. And how was he cured from his sickness by the howlers?

"Okka makka dakka yakka HA!"

Heraex walked away from the statue. "I think they're done with their little chant." Past Gold followed Heraex to the end of a branch while the present Gold walked up to the leader howler.

"How was I cured?" he asked.

The howler didn't even look down at him. "By special secret that I know. You cannot know because you are not worship Mala-mala!" the howler said; he ignored Gold's response and crawled over him into an opening in the tree.

Gold looked over his shoulder and saw the setting sun. *It must be time for bed,* he thought as he followed them into the tree. "Heraex, come on! We have to come in here. They will be insulted if we don't," he whispered. Without another word, Heraex and past Gold lifted off their feet and walked behind him. Heraex almost slipped on the branch from the rainfall that still did not end. Past Gold managed to stop her from falling by grabbing onto her back with his claws.

As he entered the tree, golden leaves brushed against him. He looked around in the tree. Even the inside was gold! The opening of the tree was filled with pulled-out grass and leaves, making a perfect entrance. From that entrance, there were eight tunnels that led to different parts of the tree. The blonde monkey went into the middle tunnel while the two guards went into the last one. Two of the other howlers escorted the three tamarins down the farthest one to the right. This was a long way down, but within every ten-tamarin feet, there was at least one opening with golden vines with leaves attached to them at the entrance. This place was surely beautiful.

As they walked through the tunnel, every few minutes Gold saw a kind of jar made from grass and woven with vines with leaves surrounding the outside. Within it, there was light. Moving light—it was alive! He watched as the weird creatures moved inside the grass jar.

"Those firebugs. They easy to catch and use them for light in this dark tree," one howler said. It seemed as if it read his thoughts about the firebugs. Although only the leader of the howlers seemed to speak good grammar, all of them got their points across. The howlers suddenly stopped at a large opening with more vines and leaves at the entrance.

"Here you sleep for night. Don't let bugs bite," the howler said in a sarcastic yet scary voice. They quickly jumped into the tunnel again and ran up to the top of the tree, again making loud howls. The howls seemed to ring throughout the whole tree.

The three tamarins looked at the entrance and quickly jumped inside. Heraex lay down on the leaf bedding. It was quite comfortable. In each corner of the room, there was one of those light jars.

"It is very nice of these creatures to let us stay here," Heraex commented. Gold agreed with her, but something bothered him about this place. With past Gold and Heraex already sleeping, he decided to also. He jumped over to a corner and lay down on the nice bedding.

"An ocelot you say stole it this time?"

Gold's eyes opened with alarm. He heard the faintest talking through a hole close to where his ear was. He looked in it, and it seemed to stretch through the tunnel. The sound must had been carried through it from the other howler's room. It sounded like the leader's voice.

"Well, I guess we have to kill it for a sacrifice too. No one steals our gold and gets away with it."

Gold was wide-awake. He couldn't believe what he was hearing. The story of the tree of gold was true. Anyone that took gold from it suffered death, and no one ever saw him or her again. Maybe these howlers had something to do with it. But going after that ocelot? Were they going sloth?

"We forgot to tell you that we sent two of our soldiers to kill it and retrieve the gold, but it didn't turn out the way it should have."

Gold listened closer.

"What do you mean by that, Trooper?"

Trooper? Is that one of their names?

"They both dead. Ocelot killed them with no trouble at all."

He heard an angry howl from the leader.

"Well, we must sacrifice something, or we will displease Mala-mala. Are you aware of that?"

He heard a reply from Trooper but couldn't make it out.

"Go to sleep. We all need it. And those tamarins, go check on them. They need to be ready for tomorrow's ceremony."

Tomorrow's ceremony? What is that supposed to mean? He heard the footsteps of the trooper as he came to the entrance of the opening. Loud breathing came closer to him as Gold pretended he was sleeping. He heard a "humph," and then the breathing faded in the distance.

Chapter 10

Ceremony

Gold woke up to chanting once again. It seemed to ring in his ears and showed no sign of going away. He still couldn't believe what he heard yesterday night. He must tell Heraex and past Gold.

"Heraex," he whispered.

"What?"

He turned to the entrance and saw her about to leave into the tunnel. "Come here. I need to tell you both something important," he directed at both of them. In the far corner, making sure no one could hear them, Gold told them what had happened.

"So they kill whoever takes the gold?" Heraex questioned.

Past Gold butted in. "And what about that ceremony for us? Weren't they supposed to sacrifice that ocelot? Now who?"

This comment sparked Gold's mind. They were going to be sacrificed! They had to be fully healed and ready for it. That's why those howlers had been so nice to them.

"Really? Do you think that's the case?" past Gold said while entering his thoughts.

"Heraex, I'll explain later. Just act like you have no idea what's going on. We'll ask them questions about how to get to the north, and then we'll escape," he said quickly. The only reason he talked fast was because a howler, Trooper, he thought, was coming to the entrance. All three of them walked to the entrance, ignoring the sound that Trooper made, meaning for them to get out.

"You have special day. We feed you delicious supper, and you please us."

Gold already knew where this was going. He just made a smile sweep across his face. All of them climbed back up the tunnel and jumped out of the entrance to the golden tree. The sun was just rising, and he saw to the left all of the howlers sitting on a branch. They all howled to the sky, next to that stupid statue. The sun was in the middle of the sky, and he saw to the left all the howlers on a branch. The howlers must have gotten them up later so they would be hungry.

Oh, figs! Do you think they might be fattening us up for something?

I think so. I know so. So just keep quiet! I'll ask questions.

Okay, just don't be too suspicious.

Gold leapt up to Trooper. "I thank you very much for the meal we'll be sharing. But after the meal, I'm afraid we will have to leave. Do you know how to get to the north from here?" Gold asked cautiously.

The monkey smirked. "Yes," he said, smiling, as if he thought they weren't going to get out. "You go west from here, and then you find a wood house."

A wood house? What is he talking about? Gold wondered. "Thank you," he said while walking to Heraex and past Gold.

The leader of the howlers jumped down from a branch. "You must get ready while we make food. Go to the room, and we will have food ready in a little bit. Trooper will come and get you when you're ready."

Without hesitation, they all scrambled down the tree into their room.

"We have to get out of here," whispered Heraex. "They are going to kill us!"

Gold wondered for a second. "I got it! You know the reading on the statue? God Mala-mala will come again for Gold? It might be . . . me." He shuddered at the word. Everything had to do something with him lately.

"You're right! Us!" past Gold said. "But how do we know what they will do to you? Both of you are here. Wouldn't that mess up their prophecy?" They sat for a second.

"No! It wouldn't because maybe that's why the god is coming. To take one of us out. There is only meant to be one Gold." Gold assured.

"But what about the sacrifice?" Heraex trailed off, realizing the sacrifice would be her and the Gold that's left.

"Uh-oh!" Gold screamed as Trooper came by.

"We ready for you!" he howled as he bounded up the tunnel in the tree.

The three of them walked up slowly as the chanting got louder. To their surprise, the statue was glowing. A whole bunch of fruit and nuts were laid out on the branches too.

"Now we eat!" The five howlers dug into their food. Gold just slowly ate a mango as Heraex took a bite out of a nut.

What do we do? One of us will be taken out of this time. Probably me because I'm not supposed to be in it, past Gold said.

Relax. We'll get through this, and you will be able to get back to your Heraex. And then you will do this all over again, but instead, you will be in my position.

I never thought of that before.

As soon as everyone was finished eating their meals, the leader of the howlers stood up and walked in front of the glowing statue. "God Mala-mala! Relocate our gold!"

Gold looked around him and saw three light rays pop up from deep in the forests. The light rays carried back the gold the ocelots had stolen. The gold landed in front of the statue and started to float in a circular motion in front of it. In the circular motion appeared the past! It showed them when Gold brought the past Gold here and kept going until it was just before that happened. The wind began to get rougher than it already was from the storm and pulled past Gold in.

"No!" Heraex grabbed his tail before he got sucked in.

"It's okay, Heraex! I need to go back! It's not my"—he went into a whispery voice—"time."

Heraex let go of his tail and watched him go closer and closer into the porthole to the past.

I'll never forget you, past Gold.

Me either. Goodbye, my friend.

Past Gold's voice trailed off in his mind as the porthole closed with past Gold inside of it.

"Now your turn!" Trooper said as he bounced toward Gold. A crackling in the bushes stopped him.

"How dare you take back my gold." The voice got clearer as the prehistoric ocelot jumped through the ferns.

"Your gold? It is not. It is Mala-mala gold!" Trooper then swung at the ocelot with his mouth opened. The ocelot put his paw up, and Trooper then smacked into it, sending him flying against the golden tree. Blood spattered as Trooper lost his life with a single blow to the face.

"Anymore?" the ocelot asked, smiling. The other four howlers lunged for him and the rest of his group. Gold watched long enough to see that the leader killed one of the members, but then blood—lots of blood—was spilled.

"We have to leave!" Heraex demanded. They both leapt off the branches and toward the west. He remembered what Trooper had told him about how to get to the north, and this was the only way he could go. With no more past Gold in his head, he began to get lonely as they bounded past the pouring rain that crashed for four weeks now. The water was now halfway up the trees on the ground. He wondered how the animals were surviving down there. With no more questions, he kept going west to find the wood house.

Chapter 11

The Wood House

After two days of traveling through the wretched rain, they finally came across a wooden structure on top of the forest canopy. The wood was unlike any found in the forest of rain, and it was drenched like they couldn't believe. Gold jumped a few branches over to it. "It smells strong and tangy."

Heraex jumped beside him. "You're right. It's unlike anything I've seen before."

Gold looked up, his eyes flinching from the rain. It was pretty big, but big enough for what? A friend or a foe?

"Let's see if there's a way into it! Maybe it'll have something in there to tell us where to go next," Gold said as he climbed up the weird-smelling wood and eventually found a hole that led inside. It was very big too, but not as big as those howlers the ocelot had probably killed. "Come here. I found a hole. If we go in it, it might give us shelter from the rain."

Heraex followed Gold through the hole. It was dark, with patches of grass, flowers, ferns, and herbs they had never seen before. "It smells good with all of these things lying here. I wonder what they are."

Gold was about to touch a flower when he heard something like footsteps. He turned around to see nothing there. "Heraex, do you know anything about this place?"

Heraex looked at Gold. "No, this part of the forest is a blur to me. I do, however, remember something about a wooden structure that was made by the shadow creatures."

Alarm busted in Gold's belly. *Great*, he thought, *another creature to try and kill us.* He heard the footsteps again.

"We're not alone!" Heraex screeched as a dark, foxlike creature bounded down from a branch in the wood house.

"I have been expecting you. Follow me." The creature croaked.

Gold guessed that he was old. He and Heraex followed the creature as they entered another level of the wooden structure. More flowers and ferns were on the ground. A light in the corner caught Gold's eye. The creature quickly snatched it in its mouth, then took out a woven basket like the ones they saw in the howlers' territory. He spit the bug into the basket and sealed it with a leaf. As it stepped into the light, Gold got a clear picture of it. It had a white face, a muzzle, a brown body, and a fluffy tail.

"What are you?" Gold said, trying to sound brave.

"I am a coati. My name is Cyndar. I have been the caretaker of this wooden house for years, and I take in flowers and other herbs and ferns to make medicines and merchandise like this woven basket for light bugs."

An idea sparked into Gold's head, but Heraex got to it first. "Did any howlers come here lately?"

The coati shivered. "Yes, and they take things by force, only to lure unsuspecting prey into their tree for sacrifices. They take my baskets and medicines too."

Gold was understanding, and then he spoke, "That's what they did to us. Don't worry though. You will never be seeing them again."

Disbelief washed over Cyndar's face. "You mean you killed them? How could two tamarins kill those seven beasts?"

Gold remembered that the leader of the howlers had sent two monkeys to fetch the gold, but the ocelot killed them both without any trouble.

"We didn't kill them." Heraex assured. "The ocelot group did. And their leader is trying to kill us too."

Gold squinted at the remark. He didn't like the idea of being wanted dead.

"I see. I have heard of only one prophecy, the only prophecy." Cyndar took the basket and put it closer to the wall, and then images were revealed. At first, there was a golden monkey, and then a black monkey, and after that, there was an ocelot.

"I have been trying to read this for years, and I have figured it out. A golden monkey, meaning you, Gold. That is your name, I presume?"

Gold nodded, and Cyndar continued, "The black monkey with a sun above it, meaning never-ending monkey, and an ocelot with a sun above it, which means never-ending ocelot. I still do not know why the sun is above these two animals."

Heraex stepped forward and told Cyndar about the stuck-in-time story.

"I don't believe it." Cyndar shrugged.

"Here, I'll show you I'm immortal!"

Gold then knew what to do. He quickly scratched Heraex in the face, her blood pouring forth. He heard Cyndar gasp, but then the blood went back into the cut, and the cut was sealed in seconds. A sigh of relief came from him.

"Oh my, this is serious. The only way to stop this ocelot is to follow the rest of the prophecy." He moved the light basket further down, and more images appeared from the light. This time it showed a tree with a sun above it, and next to it was a skull—a monkey skull!

"I do not know what this means, but I think I have an idea of some sort. Since there is a sun over the top of the tree, I'm guessing that the tree is never-ending too. But trees must die sometime too, unless they are stuck. I got it! It means the tree is the cause of this. And the skull must mean death, which means that a death on the tree must trigger its power!" It all made sense to Gold now, and it might have made even more sense to Heraex.

"So the only way to fix everything is to—"

Gold cut Heraex off. "To do the same thing."

Cyndar walked away, and then walked back after about three minutes. He came back with several gigantic leaves in his mouth. He put them all on the floor. Dust from the floor made Gold cough as the leaves hit the ground.

"These leaves are very important for they are a way around the forest of rain. You can pick whichever one you like. You are going somewhere, right?" His voice creaked.

Gold spoke up, "Yes. We are going to the north to find my family."

Cyndar lifted his head. "Then I suppose you need this one." He picked up a dark green leaf with red images on it. He smelled the leaf, and they smelled like mango. "I use juices to write with," he said while giving the map to them. "This will help you on your way. You must, however, concentrate more on how you will undo the time curse the tree has set on everyone who was affected."

Gold nodded. He knew as soon as he found his family, he would be able to help Heraex, her mom, and everyone get back to reality. Her mom! "But, Heraex! How come your mom is asleep all this time?"

Heraex smiled as if she knew how to answer the question. "Well, all of us got stuck in time from the state we were in. I was very young, my mother was unconscious, and so on."

Come to think of it, it had been four and a half weeks already since he'd started traveling with Heraex. She was still the same size while he grew bigger. He had been a bit smaller than her when they first met, and now he was at least a quarter larger than her.

"I know where the tree is. I have a map. After you find your family, you will come to the tree. We have to fix it," Cyndar said.

Gold and Heraex nodded at the coati.

"There is one more thing you will need before you continue to make this journey." Cyndar took something from a nearby branch. It looked like a jar but smaller than the ones that were used for light bugs. He took another jar out too although this one was thick while the other one was thin, and this one had straps coming down from the bottom and the top. Cyndar put it on Heraex; it fit perfectly around her arms. Cyndar opened the top and put the scrawny jar into the bigger one, and he put the map in it too. "Wouldn't this get wrecked from the rain?" Heraex asked.

"Oh, yeah! The rain! What's does the rain have to do with the prophecy?" Gold uttered. He looked at the images again and spotted a rain cloud beside the skull and another gold monkey beside the rain cloud.

"It means you're the only one who could save these creatures that are stuck. The rain will continue until you have fulfilled your duty" Cyndar said.

Gold felt more weight on his shoulders than ever even though Heraex was the one carrying the items on her back. As the three of them climbed up to the hole, he heard Cyndar say, "It will take you no longer than five days to get to you destination. If it stops raining, which it won't, you would be looking at three days." Gold didn't want to hear that.

"I will meet you at the tree! Good luck, Gold and Heraex!" Cyndar bounded away from branch to branch until the two primates couldn't see him anymore.

Gold jumped to the highest branch of the tree. He looked over to the north. "Heraex, let me see that map."

She took out the map and handed it to him. Gold looked closely; he was happy. At first, he had to cross the trees in front of him. This would be easier than he thought! "Let's go, Heraex," he said after handing her back the map. "We just need to keep going this way until I recognize something." With that, they soared across the branches, through the darkness of the storm.

Chapter 12

Flood

Gold and Heraex jumped through the forest canopy as the rain poured down heavily. "Will this rain ever stop?" Heraex blurted out.

"Not until I fix this. I'm the key," Gold said with a joking smile. Come to think of it, the rainwater was getting a lot higher. It got to about three quarters up the trees. "The water's really high! We should get to taller trees!" he said while trying to overpower the noise of the rain slamming against the trees and leaves.

"Wait! Something's not right." Heraex said. They both looked down at the water. All was silent, except the sound of raindrops. Then suddenly, a dark scaly body jumped out of the water and onto the branch before them. The scaly creature just looked at Heraex with huge dark eyes.

"Well, well, well. You couldn't get away from me that easily, primate." Its tone was directed at Heraex.

"Oh, yeah! You're that creature I was too busy to fight with a few weeks ago." Her voice was full of sarcasm.

The creature became anger; it opened his jaws and snapped at Heraex. Heraex jumped out of the way quickly but slammed into a branch. Heraex fell unconscious.

"No, Heraex!" Gold screamed as he got the creature's attention.

The creature turned. "I guess it's your turn, then I will eat both of you for supper," it said with an evil smirk. The creature lunged for him. Thinking fast, Gold swung around the branch, sending the creature straight into the water again.

"Gold, I have a plan." Gold turned. It was Heraex! Her neck was twisted around, but Gold watched her fix her neck back into place.

"Go get a stick. Break it off from something. I'll somehow get him on his belly, and that's when I'll stab. Don't worry. I'll get his attention."

Without another word, she leapt onto the branch that was closest to the creature. "Hey! Scaly butt! What's your problem? It looks like you're sick with all those bumps on you!"

Gold heard this as he looked for a good stick. He heard fighting and clamping in the background; whatever Heraex was doing, she was doing a good job of it.

He found a stick and went on top of it. He jumped as hard as he could, and the stick fell off and down on another branch. He watched as the stick quickly lost balance. Gold jumped on the branch and grabbed the stick with his teeth before it could fall into the water. He jumped a few branches higher to where Heraex was fighting the creature. Heraex jumped over the creature as it tried to snap at her. She took her nails and scratched the creature's eyes. He heard a shriek from the creature as it turned on its back while floating in the water.

"Gold! Now!"

Gold then threw the stick at the creature. The pointy edges easily pierced through the creature's thin skin. Blood floated away in the current of the water as the creature sank. He and Heraex watched until he was nowhere to be seen.

"That was a close one," Gold said.

"Yeah. I haven't fought like that in a while. So much violence."

Gold nodded in understanding. "Come on. We have to move on, and this rain isn't going to stop until we fix this." Gold pulled out the map from Heraex's pack. "It says we're close. We're really close! We could get to the north side in a few minutes," Gold said excitedly. Heraex smiled, and they both leapt a few trees to the north side.

"This must be the border to the north." He saw ferns and flowers marking a sort of line that kept going until he couldn't see it anymore. As soon as they crossed the border, it was dry! The rain hadn't passed through here yet, and the river hadn't come over here either. They both heard a roaring sound.

"Heraex?" Gold questioned.

"Hold on tight!" she screamed. Trees came tumbling down as water flowed through the whole north side. It came closer until Gold noticed that they were too low.

"Oh, no!" Gold screamed as the current pulled him away. Struggling for breath, Gold swam up to the top of the flood and took a few breaths.

He looked behind him and saw a dead-looking tree. He closed his eyes as he braced himself for the pain. The current made him crash through the dead tree; bark pieces flew everywhere as Gold yowled in pain. The water current pushed him closer to a vine. He grabbed hold of it when he was close enough. He swung over to the nearest high branch. He quickly became unconscious as the water filled his lungs.

Chapter 13

Home

Rain blurred Gold's vision as the drops washed through his golden fur. He lifted his head and saw Heraex sitting beside him, eating a mango.

"Hey. You're up," she said gleefully. Gold looked down and saw the rushing of the water.

"The water is still going?" he asked.

Heraex lifted her head. "Yep. You've been unconscious for about two hours."

He stood up in a panic. "We have to go! Hurry! We have to find my parents." He looked to the right of him and saw a tree. A familiar tree too. "That's my tree! That's my home! We found it, Heraex! We finally found it! Come on!" He quickly bounced off the branches to the tree on the right side of him. Vines shot by as he kept running, until he got to a disaster.

Gold suddenly halted. His excitement trailed off as he saw something horrible. Branches were broken off, and blood was stained on the bark. "Oh my god. This is a disaster. What happened?" Gold's mind was suddenly flooded with anger. "It was those sloth-headed ocelots! They killed my family!" Gold began to pound on the tree. Heraex's eyes began to tear.

"What's all the banging about?" A familiar voice trailed off. Gold turned around to meet a familiar face.

"Gold?"

Gold's eyes started to tear. "Dad?"

His dad nodded his head as they wrapped their tails. "Gold, I thought I would never see you again! What happened to you? The last thing we remembered was when you disappeared while looking for me." His dad let out a smile.

"I was carried away by a bird when Mom got her tail bit." Gold stopped in his tracks. A hint of worry rushed through him.

"Mom! Where is she? Is she okay?"

His dad's head went down. "Umm, Gold. Blume didn't make it."

His voice turned into squeaks. "No! That's not true!"

Jigsaw nodded his head.

"Did anyone else survive?"

Jigsaw nodded again. "About a quarter of our troop survived the attack from those vicious creatures." Jigsaw looked over at Heraex. "And who's this?"

Heraex looked up. Her eyes shimmered in the rain. "I'm Heraex. I came from the south side."

Jigsaw lifted his brow. "Very well. Come inside from this rain. It's very strange how it started just like that, eh?"

Gold and Heraex nodded simultaneously. They both followed Jigsaw inside their home. The inside was dark, still scented with the smell of blood. Gold then saw four other tamarins looking at him. Two were female and two were male.

"Let me introduce you to the rest of your family, Gold," Jigsaw said proudly.

"Gold!" he heard everyone shout. All of the monkeys jumped beside him and questioned him.

"Okay, okay. Give him some room. He just got here remember?"

All of the monkeys suddenly backed off, except for one old primate. "Welcome back, Gold." Her voice was sweet, with a hint of aging. Gold smiled from the welcome. "My name is Wave, and I'm the leader of this troop. Of what used to be this troop." Her voice seemed to have sympathy, probably for all of the tamarins that had died.

"And I'm Dew!" an excited voice shouted. It was a small tamarin. He looked like he was a newborn. Maybe at least six days old.

Wave spoke up, "Yes, that is Dew. His father died in battle, but his mom survived. She died six days ago from blood loss." Wave looked up and sighed.

Two other tamarins walked up to Gold. "Hi, Gold!" they both said. One was male, and the other was female.

"Don't you remember us?" the male said.

Gold shook his head, feeling sad that he couldn't remember.

"We're your brother and sister. I'm Amber," the female said as she looked into Gold's eyes.

Gold looked back. No wonder her name was Amber. Her eyes were the color of it.

"And this is Night," Amber said as she pointed to Gold's brother. Night nodded his head and looked away. Was that jealousy he sensed?

Wave cleared her throat. "Since you two are staying now, we should get you two some rooms."

Gold shifted. "Actually,"—everyone looked at Gold—"we have to go back to the southern part of the forest of rain." A huge gasp came from each of the primates.

Wave looked at the crowd. "Everyone leave. I could tell something private must be discussed. Jigsaw, you may stay."

Jigsaw turned around and approached them. "Why do you have to leave so soon? You just got back, and we thought you would stay."

Concern swept through Wave.

"Well, it's a long story."

Jigsaw looked at Gold. "I've got all the time in the world."

Heraex looked up. "Actually, I do."

Gold felt amusement swivel up his fur. Wave and Jigsaw just watched, puzzled.

"Show them, Heraex."

Heraex picked up a twig on the ground and stabbed herself in the chest.

"No!" Wave cried.

Jigsaw watched in amazement as Heraex pulled out the stick, and her eyes became white. The whiteness disappeared, and her regular eye color came back. The blood reversed itself and went back into her body. Her skin attached back together as her fur grew back where the twig cut it.

"Oh my god!" Wave exclaimed. "I don't understand. How?"

Gold sat them down and told them the whole story about the curse, his adventure, and his dreams.

"You have the dreams too?" Jigsaw suddenly asked.

Gold was shocked. "You mean, I'm not the only one?" His voice shuddered.

"No, your mother, Blume, had this ability. She said she could travel to the future with this ability."

This was amazing! That's where he got this ability. But he could only travel through the past and bring people back as far as he knew. Actually, he never tried to go to the future.

"No," Jigsaw said. Gold and Heraex looked up. "I'm not letting you leave again." Gold was shocked. This was his destiny.

"But I must go! The forest of rain depends on me!"

Jigsaw nodded his head. "Then I'm coming with you."

Gold's heart danced. "Okay," he said.

Wave spoke, "Okay, since that is settled, you must get some rest. I will inform the rest of the colony." Wave jumped away to where Gold's siblings and the newborn went.

"Come on," Jigsaw said as he brought them to their rooms. They went down a narrow hallway until they came to the first room. "Here you go, Heraex. This will be your room for tonight." Heraex nodded and padded in.

"Heraex!" Gold shouted. He saw Heraex turn around. "We leave tomorrow, so be up when the sun rises." Heraex nodded and went into the room.

"Your room is just up there," Jigsaw said as he pointed to a room far up the wooden hallway. The stench of blood still caused Gold to flinch. "Are you okay?" Jigsaw was concerned.

"Yeah, I just—never mind."

Jigsaw gave a worried look and walked away. Gold trotted into a hollow room. *There's nothing in here*, Gold thought. He quickly lay down and fell into dreamland.

Chapter 14

Third Time's the Charm

The wind blew against Gold's fur. Branches flew as the rain poured harder than ever. A branch suddenly hit Gold in the face, making him lose his balance. His tail wrapped around a branch, but it was too late, he fell into the river. Water rushed into his lungs as he sank into the water. He swam up to the surface, coughing for air. When he spit, red flew out. Was he bleeding? He looked down into the river and saw red. The whole river was stained with blood. He looked to the side of him and saw a body float up. He swam over to it while struggling against the current.

He turned it over and saw Cyndar, the old coati who helped him find his home. Something suddenly touched his feet. He let out a yelp as he swam away from it. Another body floated up. As the face became clearer and clearer, he saw that it was Jigsaw. "No!" Gold screamed. He kept looking down into the river. Three shadows started to rise from the bottom and quickly floated up to the surface. He recognized his siblings as their faces became visible. The third one was Wave. Gold screamed up at the sky. A sudden wave crushed at his head as it passed. Behind it, a vicious face appeared.

It was the ocelot. Blood dripped from its fangs as it came closer. The sharp fangs dug into his neck, causing him to look up. He saw the sky and saw other monkeys! Three other bodies became visible as they dropped from the trees—Heraex's, Dew's, and one he did not recognize splashed into the blood-colored river. Red blinded him when the ocelot bit through his skin. His vision started to fade away.

Sunlight scorched Gold's eyes when they opened. He listened to himself shift from right to left. He did have to get up though; he, Heraex, and Jigsaw were leaving today. He heard a knock at the side of the bark. It was Jigsaw telling him to get up. Gold sprang up, still thinking of the horrific dream. Were his powers growing? Was it a dream of the future? One thing was for sure though, something wasn't right, and he would get to the bottom of it. He walked out the entrance to his room and met Jigsaw.

"Come on, Gold. Get ready. We have to go soon. Go get Heraex, and get her ready for the departure. I'll go and get breakfast ready." With that, he walked off to the entrance of the meeting hall. The meeting hall was where the entire colony got together and announced certain things like mourning deaths and celebrating births.

Gold bounced away into Heraex's room. He peeked his head in while the sunlight crept through the holes in the bark. To his surprise, Heraex was already up.

"Hey, we have to go down for breakfast. We have to go soon and fix everything before it gets worse."

Heraex turned her head toward him, tears falling down her face.

"But that's the thing. What if you don't survive? I know I will, but if you die, I will be doomed to this life without dying forever! Everyone I love would die, and I will still be here. It's not right."

Her sudden outburst made Gold twitch. He never knew she felt so strongly about it before. Should he tell her about his dream right now—about finding everyone's lifeless body in a river stained red with blood. Gold shook his head, thinking about his own thoughts. He wouldn't tell her, not yet.

Gold remembered the other startling dream he had about Heraex about a month ago. He remembered how Heraex turned around and suddenly turned into that ocelot. The ocelot had her dead in its mouth, its eyes bright red. Shaking it away for Heraex, he moved closer, trying to make Heraex feel better.

"Gold?" Heraex said in a sad voice.

"Yeah?" he replied.

"Thank you so much for helping me find out how I got stuck in this mess."

Gold went a little bit closer. "You're welcome. After all, you are my best friend." They both smiled at each other and rushed downstairs to eat breakfast. He and Heraex both climbed down a narrow passageway to the entrance of the meeting hall. When they arrived, everyone welcomed them with joy and happiness.

"Welcome to breakfast, Gold and Heraex," he heard Wave shout out. Their breakfast looked very delicious. It might be his best meal since the feast at the howlers' place. The thought of the howlers made Gold shiver.

He never wanted to see those evil monkeys again, and he didn't think he would. The ocelot gang killed them. He did see the prehistoric one kill Trooper with one paw blow.

The smell of the food made Gold snap out of his trancelike state. All of the food looked delicious. He looked from the corner of his eye and saw Heraex digging into an orange. Gold sniffed the food. It smelled like figs, oranges, and some other food he couldn't recall. He slowly picked it up with his nails. It was very hard and looked like a dried-up orange, but it was a brown color. It also had a chalky smell. It had something in it too.

Wave must have seen him examining the food because she spoke up, "Those are called cocoa beans. They are very delicious and have a great taste to them. It's a little hard when you bite into it, but it's worth it."

Thankful for the information, he quickly bit into the cocoa bean. Wave was right. It was very delicious! Within a few seconds, he devoured the whole cocoa bean, then decided to have another. He had never seen cocoa beans on his journey yet. Gold decided to take five cocoa beans and asked Heraex to put them in her pack. She agreed and did what Gold told her. Shortly, after everyone was done eating, Wave stood up and raised her hands. Everyone looked, even the newborn, Dew.

"When are they leaving?" Dew shouted in a sad voice. "I want them to stay so they could play with me!"

Wave silenced him with a whip of her tail through the air.

"Since Gold, Heraex, and Jigsaw are leaving, we should be proud of them. I still do not understand the whole thing that Gold and Heraex are telling us, but I definitely believe them. And with that, I wish them good luck on their journey."

After she said her speech, everyone started to cheer. Gold felt a feeling he had never felt before. He felt happy, proud, scared, and enthusiastic at the same time. Gold couldn't help but smile. He looked over at Heraex, and she was smiling at all of the cheering monkeys.

Jigsaw then stood up. "Okay, Heraex, Gold. Let's go. We have a curse to lift."

Gold knew he was serious, but he couldn't help but find a hint of a joke in Jigsaw's words. They both stood up and walked over to join Jigsaw. Jigsaw's blue eyes shimmered in the morning sun. "Heraex, take out the map. Maybe it will tell us how to get to the south side."

"Here it is," Heraex announced as she pulled it out.

Gold took the map and looked at it. "This is no use. It doesn't tell us how to get to the south side." Gold saw Heraex get a sparkle in her eye.

"Wait a second. Turn the page over," she said.

He swiftly turned it over, and he could see more writing and more images eventually leading toward the south side.

"Good old Cyndar. I knew he wouldn't leave us hanging."

Jigsaw turned around. "Cyndar?"

Gold suddenly remembered he had left the part of Cyndar out of the adventure he told to his father.

"He was just a friend who's helping us along the way. He's the one who's actually meeting us at the time tree to guide us on how to fix the curse."

Jigsaw nodded and suddenly spoke, "Okay, let's go."

Chapter 15

Departure

The slamming rain slid off the leaves as Gold drank from them. The drops on the leaves were delicious. At least one good thing came out of this cursed rain. Heraex was beside him, watching him drink.

"When's your father going to come out? We've been waiting here for about twenty minutes!"

Gold finished his last slurp before he put his head up. "My dad's coming soon. Don't worry. He will be here. And take that map out again. I want to see where our first landmark is to get to the south."

Heraex slipped the bag off her back and set it down on a branch. She opened it and grabbed the map. The first image on the map was a circular part of the forest. It looked like vines wrapped around every tree.

"It shouldn't take us long to get there." Heraex nodded as her ears twitched from the sound coming through the entrance of the tree. It was Jigsaw making his way through the rough bark.

"Are we ready to go?"

Both of them nodded.

"Okay then, let's go."

They all leapt through the trees down to the south. About ten minutes into the journey, Jigsaw turned to Gold while they were running through the trees. "So what's our first destination?"

Heraex jumped in the middle of them. Gold lost his balance and tripped over his own feet but righted himself in a second.

Gold gave her an annoyed look as he answered the question, "We're going to a part in the forest where the trees are in circles. A lot of vines are on the trees too and stuff." His voice echoed in his head. It was getting a bit awkward with his father beside him all the time. He couldn't just talk to Heraex anymore. *Why couldn't I have mind chat with her?* He thought desperately.

As Gold got closer and closer to the first landmark, he couldn't help but hear a sharp sound. It got louder the closer he got. "What's that sound?" he asked Heraex.

Heraex stopped running and listened carefully. "I don't know what that is." Her voice was speckled with worry.

"Only one way to find out," his father said and leapt through the tree branches. Gold then heard a gasp from his father's direction. Even though his gasp was covered by rain splatter, he could still make out a few breaths.

"Father!" Gold rushed through the leaves to where his father was sitting. "What's wrong?" Gold's voice trailed off as he looked in front of him. The circular forest that was supposed to be there just wasn't! It was replaced by flat ground, and these creatures were taking the trees down! What did they want with them? That was someone's home! How could they take that?

Gold saw Heraex run up to him from the corner of his eye. What were those things? Before Gold could ask out loud, Heraex answered his question.

"Shadow creatures!" Her voice was full of anger.

"Shadow creatures? What do you mean? What do they want?" Jigsaw asked in concern.

"They only want one thing, our trees! They take them for some reason, and then they take them back in these weird creatures that roll." They all stared in awe. The creatures had no fur except for some on their heads. They had no tails, and they had smooth colored leaflike things on them.

"Those things are hideous!" Jigsaw screeched.

"Shhh. We don't want them to see us and take us just like the trees." Heraex kept looking at the shadow creatures. "How are we going to get around those things?" she finally said. "Maybe if we take a detour around the shadow creatures," Gold said.

"Wait! I hear something." Gold heard Heraex say. Heraex's pointing tail told Gold that he needed to listen to the shadow creatures.

"It sounds like—"

Jigsaw cut him off. "Animals!"

Gold adjusted his vision and saw something moving. They looked like birds, and beside them looked like monkeys and other four-legged creatures. They were all crammed inside different cagelike boxes and were on those rolling creatures that the shadow creatures seemed to command.

"We have to save those poor animals!" Gold cried.

Heraex smiled. "And I just might have a plan," she said with a big grin. Jigsaw and Gold looked at her in confusion.

"What's your plan?" Gold asked.

Heraex took in a deep breath. "We need someone as bait. Then, when they capture one of us, another one of us could go and get something to break the cage!" Gold nodded. "But remember, the one who goes and gets the thing to break the cage cannot be seen by anyone."

Jigsaw stood up. "I'll do it! I'll get the object to break the cage."

Heraex nodded and spoke, "I'll be the bait."

Gold felt depressed for a second. "What do I do?" he asked.

"You could go examine the cages, but remember, don't be seen," Heraex said.

With that, all three of them bounced off the trees and into the circular clearing. Heraex ran into the middle and started to jump and make screeching sounds near the cages. Gold saw about five shadow creatures rush for Heraex. One carried a net, and the other one carried this kind of stick. Two of the shadow creatures were in a rolling creature but ran out as soon as they heard about Heraex.

He looked at the rolling creature and saw Jigsaw run inside of it, looking for something to break the cages with. Since a lot of the shadow creatures were occupied trying to get Heraex, this would be the perfect time to go and inspect the cages. As the rain smashed down, Gold looked at the cages. They were made of some heavy substance. It was impossible to break through. He looked at it more closely.

The screams of the animals within the cages distracted him from time to time. "You're going to get caught! They will take you to where things never escape! Help us!"

He kept hearing that over and over from these different creatures. When he looked down, he discovered a hole. It was small too; his nail could fit in it. He heard a screech from in front of him. It was Heraex!

Chapter 16

Catch and Release

Blood spattered on the ground as the stick poked Heraex in her side. The shadow creatures surrounded Heraex. Gold saw the blood on the ground come back into the cut on Heraex's side. He looked up at the shadow creatures and saw them back up in confusion and surprise. They suddenly got grins on their faces and caught Heraex with that net. That's exactly what had to be done. Their plan was working!

Gold looked at the cages again. He tried to fit his finger in one of the locks. The cage that he stuck his nail in seemed to turn and open. "It worked! Okay, go on, get out of here!" he said to one animal that was in the cage. The four-legged animal stuck its head out of the cage. Its white horns were sharp and poked out of the cage from its head. Its body was brown, and it had white stripes. It ran off, leaving the cage empty.

He saw one of the shadow creatures run after it. After a few seconds, the shadow creature realized it was too fast and gave up. He looked over again at Heraex. The shadow creature with the net had Heraex in it. It was walking closer to the cage Gold was next to. He quickly hid behind the nearest rolling creature. He watched as the shadow creature violently shoved Heraex inside the cage where the hoofed animal was before Gold set it free. It locked the cage and walked away.

The distraction was over, and Jigsaw was still in the rolling creature. *We don't need anything to break the cage if we can use our nails.* Gold thought. He jumped to where Heraex's cage was and got her attention.

"Gold! Did you see that? I made a good distraction, eh?"

Gold quickly put his nail in the hole and turned it. The cage turned open, and Heraex was free. "Okay, we have to get these other animals free," Heraex said.

Heraex swung out of the cage. "So you just use your nail? And what about Jigsaw? We need to help him!" Heraex screamed.

"Shhh. We don't want any attention drawn toward us. We don't want any of these creatures to get us. And yes, you put your nail in the hole and turn it to the left. We will get Jigsaw as soon as these animals are free. He can handle himself right now."

Heraex nodded and rushed toward the nearest cage. It took her a while to get the right grip, but she eventually got it opened. The cage that she opened had many different kinds of birds in it. They all were colorful, and some had weird designs. A few light blue birds flew out of the cage and went toward the trees. Heraex told them to let out less sounds when they flew away. It didn't catch much of the shadow creatures' attention. They were too busy digging with their sticks with flat rocks on them and cutting down the trees.

Gold saw Heraex run to another cage with another animal like Cyndar in it. Gold ran to a big cage with an animal that looked like the one he let out earlier, but it was skinnier, had a longer neck, shorter horns, and longer legs. It had a young next to it, which meant that the animal was a mother. The white markings on its face were illuminated in the rain, making the creature look even more scared. He took his nail and unlocked the cage. The creature looked surprised but grateful at the same time.

"Thunk gene," it whispered in a different language. Gold guessed it must have meant thank you.

He watched the two animals run off to where the forest started. He looked to the left of him and saw Heraex open another cage with a type of bird with a brightly colored beak inside. Its beak was huge, and every time it opened, it seemed to swallow the whole forest. About five of them lifted their wings and headed toward the forest. Gold looked around and saw four more cages with animals in them screaming for help. This got the shadow creatures' attention. About six of them ran for Heraex and Gold with big nets. At least this got the attention off Jigsaw. Where was he anyway?

He then ran to another cage with a giant type of rodent in it. He had seen other rodents like mice and other things like that before, but this one was huge! It was about half the size of the hoofed animal he set free earlier. Under pressure, he quickly unlocked the cage and set the two giant rodents free. They ran for their lives as the shadow creatures tried to get them. The shadow creatures were too slow and tripped on their feet. *What a clumsy species.* He thought to himself.

He looked as Heraex set free more birds into the forest. This plan was working perfectly, except for the part that the shadow creatures were running after them! Gold did a flip on the next cage and speedily set the next animal free. It was very slow at getting out of the cage. It dragged itself slowly over the clearing and into the forest. *How could an animal be so slow?* Shaking himself out of his thoughts, Gold ran over to help Heraex fend off the shadow creatures.

"Gold! How do I set the animals free? I couldn't find anything to break it with!" he heard Jigsaw shout. He was okay!

"You put your nail in the hole and turn it to the left!" Gold shouted back. Jigsaw did what Gold said and set an animal free. The animal ran as fast as it could to the other side of the forest. When Jigsaw watched the animal run away, Gold noticed one of the shadow creatures sneak up on Jigsaw. Before Gold could scream at him, the shadow creature scooped him up in a net.

"No!" Gold screamed.

The shadow creature swiftly shoved Jigsaw inside a cage and lifted the cage up. The shadow creature brought the cage to one of these rolling creatures and put it inside! It then commanded the rolling creature to start growling. The rolling creature started to exhale dark fumes. It rolled away with Jigsaw in it. Gold started to run after the creature.

"Dad!" he screamed as he ran faster to get to the creature. He ran up behind the creature and yelled louder, "Dad! No! Come back!" He saw Jigsaw inside the creature screaming for help. He put his hand on the inside of the creature. Gold could have sworn he heard a faint cry.

"Son, it's okay! Go fix the curse and set everything back to normal. Just go!" That was the last thing he heard from his father before he disappeared into the rain. The rain messed up the trail the creature had left.

"Dad," he whispered. "I'll find you and bring you back."

More shadow creatures running after him interrupted his thoughts. He saw Heraex run in front him. "Come on! We don't have much time!"

Gold ran behind Heraex and into the forest. They were safe now since the shadow creatures had given up chasing after them. Gold climbed up a tree and sat on a branch. The water lapped at his feet as he sobbed on the branch. Heraex climbed up and sat beside him.

"It's okay," she whispered into Gold's ear.

"I know it is." This reply surprised Heraex. "He told me it was okay to leave him there. He told me to go ahead and fix the curse before it got any worse."

Heraex smiled. "He's a good father," she said while still smiling.

"I know," Gold said while smiling back.

"So where do we go next?" Heraex pulled out the map from her pack. Gold looked at it closely. It looked like a mountain, but it wasn't as big as one. "It's called a volcano." Gold looked at Heraex, puzzled. "A volcano is like a mountain, but when it erupts, this very hot substance called lava comes out of it and burns anything in its path."

Gold started to look scared. Heraex giggled a little bit. A volcano surely wasn't a laughing matter.

"Don't worry. Volcanoes don't erupt every day, but maybe every thousand years. The last time one erupted was about three thousand years ago."

Gold felt a little bit of relief flood through him. "Okay, then let's go to the volcano!"

Chapter 17

The Volcano

Gold and Heraex rushed through the trees, closer and closer to the volcano. The rain still got harder every day, and if it didn't stop, the forest of rain would drown.

"It's getting hotter," Gold spoke to Heraex.

"Well, of course. We are getting closer to the volcano. Volcanoes are hot, and it gets more humid when you get closer."

Gold was still rushing through the rain when Heraex stopped dead in her tracks. "What's wrong?" Gold asked.

"I think we are closer than we think." Gold saw Heraex looking out of an opening through the trees. Beyond the opening, it was foggy all throughout the forest.

"I'm guessing that the volcano's around here?" Gold asked.

"Yeah. Since the rain won't stop, the volcano's lava, mixed with the rain, must have made the fog. It's pretty thick too."

Gold agreed with a nod of his head. "How will we get through? I mean, the volcano must be close if all of this fog is here."

Heraex stood up as if she knew something. "Hey! Remember that thing Cyndar gave us? It looked like a jar, and he said it might help us on our way." Heraex slipped the bag off once again and took out the little green jar. "I wonder what it is."

"Open it and find out."

Heraex bit the top off with her teeth and threw the top away. The jar suddenly began to glow, and purple smoke came out of the jar.

"Great. More fog. Just what we need," Gold stated sarcastically.

"Just wait," Heraex said. The purple smoke suddenly began to go around in circles until it started to look like a twister. It suddenly started to suck all of the fog into the purple smoke, until the fog turned purple itself. All of the purple smoke suddenly disappeared along with the fog.

"At least Cyndar knows what to do," Gold said while laughing.

"Do you think he's already there?" Gold asked.

"I'm not sure. He might be. But that is a good enough reason to get there faster." Gold started to run through the opening in the trees and toward where the fog cleared.

"Does it say we have to go around the volcano or through the volcano?" Gold asked while they rushed closer to it. The ferns brushed against Gold's face as he waited for Heraex's answer.

"The map says that we should go around it. There's no way of getting through it unless you want to become a fried tamarin from falling into the volcano."

That was one thing Gold didn't agree with, becoming a fried tamarin. He kept rushing through the forest until both of them reached the volcano. It was much larger than either of them expected.

"Wow!" Gold screeched. "It's really hot here. I don't know how any animal could live here without getting burned up."

Heraex looked up at the volcano. "I know. The sooner we get away from it, the better. I don't know about you, but I don't want to keep Cyndar waiting. He'll probably bite our heads off," she said sarcastically.

Her remark suddenly made Gold think about the dream he had a few days ago. The stench of blood filled his nostrils as the horrific images reminded him of the bloodthirsty ocelot. No one even knew his name to begin with. "I want to know more about the ocelot." It was getting darker, and the moon appeared in the sky.

"Well, the ocelot's name is Oxalamar. He usually stalks his victim and learns every single step of his opponent. He is a very dangerous creature who will stop at nothing to kill."

The ocelot's name even sounded scary. *Oxalamar.* The name gave chills to Gold. "It's getting late. I think that we should stay here until morning."

"So, any dreams lately that you should be telling me about?" Heraex asked suddenly.

Gold felt anxiety prickle up his spine. "Um, no. Not yet," he lied. Heraex gave him a nod and climbed up the nearest tree. It had lots of fruit in it, which was good because they hadn't eaten since they were at Gold's tree.

Gold followed her up the tree and bit a fruit from one of the branches. As he bit into it, juice spilled from his mouth and on the ground. This journey so far had taken the life right out of him. He was tired like he couldn't believe. After he was done eating the fruit, he slowly rested his head on the branch he was sitting on. "Good night, Heraex," he said quietly.

"Good night, Gold," she whispered back.

With that, he drifted into dreamland beside the volcano.

Chapter 18

Shadow Hunters

The next day, Gold woke up. The fog started to come back again. It was nothing but a light blanket though. They could get through it easily. He sat up and saw Heraex looking at the volcano, about one tail length away from them.

"What are you looking at?" he asked nervously because she wore a scared expression on her face.

"You see that symbol? Right there?"

Gold nodded, wondering what was so important about that symbol.

"That wavy line means that danger is here, and the arrow crossing it means that this is someone's territory," Heraex continued.

Gold then got the same scared expression Heraex had a few seconds ago. "We have to hurry up and get out of here before anything finds us," Gold said.

Gold turned around and was about to leave when he started to hear a weird sound. It sounded like the shadow creatures. "Oh, no! More shadow creatures?" he said with fear in his voice.

"No. Not quite." Heraex said as she looked over deep inside the forest. The yelling got louder until shadow creatures emerged. They didn't look like the shadow creatures they had just faced. Their skin was darker, and they had facial markings. Some were red and other markings had many different colors. There were also different symbols. They had pointy sticks too, but these sticks were nothing like the ones that the other shadow creatures had. As the creatures came closer, Gold could see that there were pieces of bones pierced through their faces. There were only about five of the shadow creatures, but they looked like they didn't want anyone in their territory. They were rushing toward Gold and Heraex.

"Watch out!" Heraex screamed as the shadow creatures threw their sticks. A stick with a sharp stone at the end almost hit Gold, but he ducked in time. The stick stuck into the branch where Gold ducked. A sigh of relief came from Gold.

"I know what they are now!" Heraex said while dodging a stick.

"You could share anytime!" Gold screamed sarcastically as he jumped to a higher branch.

"They are shadow hunters! They hunt animals and kill them for their own needs! Come on. We have to get out of here!" Heraex jumped from one tree and on to another.

"Heraex! Watch out!" Gold screeched as a stick flew right for Heraex. Before Heraex could do anything, the stick snagged the bag with the map in it and stuck it to the tree. Gold rushed for it, but another stick dove for him. The stick pierced through his finger and left it bleeding.

"Gold! Leave it! It can't be worth more than your life!"

Gold then dodged another stick and rushed for Heraex. They both ran through the trees faster than they ever had before until they could no longer hear the shadow hunters.

"We need that bag, Gold! We can't go any farther without it!"

Gold couldn't help but grin at this remark. "Then we'll get it back," he said darkly. He had a feeling Heraex liked this idea.

"Okay," she said with a smile.

"But how do you know the shadow creatures took it?" Gold asked.

"Believe me. Those stupid creatures take anything they can get their hands on," Heraex replied with a broken smile.

Gold still had a question though. "How will we find the shadow hunters' camp?"

Heraex suddenly poked her hand at the sky. "You see that smoke coming up from the trees?" Heraex asked. Gold nodded. "Well, that's where their camp is. They use fire to cook things they find."

A wave of anxiety washed through Gold. "Will they burn our bag?" Gold asked, concerned.

"No, probably not. They wouldn't burn anything that they can't eat."

Gold then climbed up a tall tree to get a better look at the shadow hunters. They were well away. It would take them at least ten minutes to get there. He could still hear the sound the shadow hunters made when they were attacking them. "Come on, Heraex! Let's go get our stuff back!"

Heraex then climbed up the tree. Barks flew off as she stabbed each piece. Gold had never noticed this before, but her nails were incredibly sharp. She could easily hurt an enemy. Gold shook himself out of his thoughts and went after Heraex. He could feel the air getting hotter as they came closer to the volcano. The smoke began to get thicker, and Gold realized that the fog was starting to come back since the rain was still pouring down. Heraex stopped with her hand out, forcing him to stop too.

"Be quiet, and look down. We don't want to risk being seen again," she whispered.

Gold looked down and saw many shadow creatures circling around the fire. The smoke went up in a large funnel toward the sky. The shadow hunters were also talking in a different language. Gold scanned up and down for the bag.

"I found it!" Heraex whispered excitedly.

"Where? I can't see it."

Heraex pointed at one of the shadow creatures. It was sitting against a tree inspecting the bag. "If that stupid creature tosses it around anymore, it's going to be in pieces!" Heraex said sarcastically.

"How will we get it?" he asked. Gold looked at Heraex and saw her looking at a tree. He guessed that she was probably looking for any possible way to get down and snag the bag without the shadow creature noticing.

"I'll go down that vine at the side of the tree!" she announced. "Then I will take the bag, and we will run for our lives."

Gold thought the plan was pretty good. "I'll stay here in case anything happens. I could tell you if anything goes wrong with a screech, okay?"

Heraex nodded and used her powerful back legs to spring across a twenty-foot clearing and to the tree where the shadow hunter was sitting. Gold's eyes wandered over to the fire. Something smelled like it was dead. And it was. A dead animal was placed on a stick and was turned over the fire every three minutes. He guessed their food would be ready for them soon. That would be the perfect chance for Heraex to climb down the vine and snatch the bag. Waiting impatiently, Gold tapped his claws on the wood. Would they ever eat? Surely, the animal was cooked enough.

Suddenly, a shadow hunter started to bang two sticks together really loudly. All of the other shadow hunters got up from where they were and walked over to the dead animal over the fire. He watched them take the animal off the stick and drop it on the ground. Then it was suddenly a free-for-all. All of the shadow hunters dropped to their knees and started to rip pieces of flesh off the cooked animal, as if they hadn't eaten in days. *Heraex better hurry up. They will be done soon.* He saw Heraex look over at him from a distance. Gold gave the nod for her to grab the bag.

She swiftly rode down the vine and on the ground where the bag lay. Gold saw the flames in the corner of his eye, flickering from the rain that was pouring down. They did have the fire under a fair amount of shelter so it wouldn't go out. Maybe they were smarter than he thought. He jumped as Heraex dropped the bag beside him. "How did you get back here so fast?"

Heraex had a scared expression on her face. Surely, it wasn't the shadow hunters because they were too busy eating. "Well, let's just say I had a pump of adrenaline!" she said with fear in her voice. She then looked in the direction of the volcano.

Chapter 19

Eruption

Gold looked around the clearing as the shadow hunters all looked up at the volcano and started to yell and run around in circles. He saw the leaves starting to shake the rainwater off them. It was just before dusk, and the volcano was already getting harder to see. The rumbling of the earth began to get stronger, and the air began to get hotter.

"What's happening?" Gold panicked.

"The volcano's erupting! Hurry we have to run!" Heraex screamed.

Without thinking, Gold ran to the top of the tree and watched the volcano. The hot liquid Heraex called lava sprouted from the top of the volcano. Rocks flew out from the top and landed around Gold. He saw one boulder fall on one of the shadow hunter's heads. Blood spilled from the hunter's head as he lay on the ground.

"This is terrible!" Gold shouted. He looked up at the volcano. He watched in fear as he saw the lava pouring down the mountain. In a few minutes, this whole clearing would be obliterated. The bright red lava covered rocks and grass as it slid down the volcano. He looked down at the shadow hunters once again and was surprised to see that five hunters died from the shooting debris. The rest were huddled in a cave next to a tree. If they didn't move soon, they would be burned by the lava or even killed.

"Hey, what's that?" Heraex asked suddenly from their view of the clearing. A tiny crystal sparkled through the mist. "We should get it!"

Gold thought that Heraex was crazy. "What do you mean?"

Heraex looked at him with a dull look. "It's going to be burned anyway, so we might as well get it." This made sense. "Okay, but you're coming with me this time. I'm not going to be alone."

Gold nodded, jumped off the top of the tree, and landed hard on the ground below them. The impact made him wince when he landed. He quickly ran over to the crystal and inspected it. "It has a weird type of symbol in it."

This made Heraex rush over to him. "Wait a second." Her voice trailed off as she looked toward the volcano once again. She looked as if she was in shock.

"Heraex?" Gold questioned as he waved his hand in her face. He directed his face to where Heraex was looking. The lava was coming down the mountain faster than they had thought. It was now bubbling at the bottom of the volcano and headed straight for them!

"Heraex, what do we do?"

Heraex suddenly snapped out of her trancelike state. "I know where I've seen that crystal before," she whispered to herself. "Gold, hurry! Grab the crystal!" she shouted at him.

He rapidly picked up the purple crystal and gave it to Heraex.

"Hurry, grab on to it with me!"

Gold followed orders and put his hands firmly on the bright-colored crystal.

"We want to go to the south side of the forest of rain!" she shouted into the air. The lava suddenly disappeared in front of them. The shadow hunters disappeared and were replaced by leaves. Rain still continued to pour from the sky. It was no longer hot either. It was just like the scenery changed altogether.

"Heraex! What just happened?" Gold demanded.

Heraex then put the purple crystal down on a branch and moved closer to Gold. "That crystal is called the teleporting crystal. I have heard of it before but had never seen it. The crystals are usually bright purple, with a type of fire burning inside."

Gold looked down at the crystal and eventually saw that what he thought was a symbol was actually a light blue flame burning inside.

"What does the fire do?" He could hardly believe that the small crystal could do so much. Then again, anything is possible in this new world.

"The burning flame in this crystal represents its power. You could use it as long as the flame doesn't die out. I don't know how the shadow hunters got to it, but they must have used it a lot. It looks like there is only one more teleport left in it."

Gold was still confused about how this managed to get here. Who made it? Who had enough power to make it? Gold climbed up a tree and saw smoke rising to the sky a long way from where they were. "We traveled a long way!" he yelled to Heraex down below. She didn't reply.

He looked around all of the scenery and realized something. When Heraex teleported them, she told the crystal to take them back to the south side. So did that mean that they were finally there? He jumped down to tell Heraex. Before he could say anything, Heraex spoke.

"We're at my home!" Heraex said excitedly.

He realized that they were at the tree where he met Heraex for the first time. He looked below him and saw the broken branch where he fell off. It was hard to believe that was almost two months ago. He suddenly heard a voice, interrupting his thoughts. It was Cyndar! He had some kind of limp as he walked toward them. As he came closer, Gold realized that he was limping because he had a huge gash on his leg. A little bit of blood leaked through his skin each time he walked.

"I see you have finally made it," Cyndar said in an excited yet scolding tone.

"What happened?" Heraex screamed, worry in her voice. She ran up to Cyndar and looked at his wounds. "It looks like claw marks. What happened to you, Cyndar?" she asked with concern.

"It's that ocelot! He attacked me when I was halfway here. He'll be here. Don't you worry about that!" he told them in a crackling voice.

Heraex and Gold both looked at each other in concern. *How will we beat this ocelot?* He wondered. Gold had a feeling Heraex had the same thought.

"Why did he attack you? How did he know that you were with us?" Heraex questioned him.

"Well, you see, he attacked me because he knew I was with you. He also told me that he has been keeping an eye on all of us for some time now."

Gold suddenly remembered the story Heraex had told him about the ocelot, that it stalks its victims until it knows how to kill them. This made him shiver. Gold imagined the sharp fangs of the ocelot sinking into his neck flesh.

"This is getting serious," said Heraex.

Cyndar nodded and looked at Gold. "It's up to you. You're the only one who can stop this rain and fix this curse so Heraex can move on."

Heraex suddenly felt a shock go right through her. "What do you mean, so I can move on?"

Cyndar let out a long sigh. "Well, when the curse is lifted, you are a normal tamarin again. If you think about it, many other animals that died a million years ago are turned into ash and dust. I'm afraid that when that curse is lifted, you will be nothing more than a normal million-year-old dead tamarin."

Heraex's eyes were wide open. She never thought that she would die when the curse was lifted! She turned to Gold. "I don't want to die," she said to him with tears falling down her face.

Chapter 20

Oxalamar

The rain poured down from the sky and to the river that seemed to get higher with every water droplet.

"The river is getting higher," a voice said from the darkness.

"But, boss, how will we get to the tamarins? We lost them when they ran away from the shadow hunters." A paw with sharp nails suddenly came out of the blackness and scraped the other creature in the face, leaving blood streaming down its face.

"I believe I will ask the questions around here," Oxalamar said calmly. He walked into the moonlight, making his face visible. There was a scar across his left eye, and both his eyes were a dark blue color. As his whole body stepped out of the shadows, five other ocelots were visible. This band of ocelots was ready to kill.

"Everyone follow me. If you find meal, you may kill it and eat it. You must keep up. If you don't, you will be punished." No one could ever tell what Oxalamar was thinking or what he would do next. They followed him up a tree where he sat and looked at the moon. His tiny spotted body was illuminated in the moonlight.

"This rain isn't going to stop. Just a few more days and the whole rain forest will be flooded, and almost nothing will be living," he said with a smirk. "I need three of my group to stay here and make sure nothing comes on this tree. If anything comes on beside any of our group members, kill it." He continued with a deep breath. "The two of you,"—he looked at two ocelots with sharp eyes—"you must go seek out Panthra. She is a very skillful predator, and I will need her as a guard. If she says no, then bribe her with power. She will then come to me."

With that, the two ocelots jumped down to the bottom of the tree they were on and ran toward Panthra's territory. The rest of the guards stayed in the tree and watched to see if anyone would dare climb up. Oxalamar then walked into a hollow opening and lay down. He heard a sudden noise.

"Hey! This is our tree! Get out!" The tiny creature lunged for Oxalamar. Oxalamar put his paw where the creature was landing and pierced it in the throat.

"Anyone else?" he asked, hoping that he could kill more. Suddenly, all ten of the creatures in the tree tried to escape, but they weren't fast enough. Oxalamar grabbed all of their tails and sunk his claws into them. Screams of pain came from the little creatures.

"Let us go! Please! We will give you our tree. Just please let us go!" a female screamed.

Oxalamar lifted the female up with his paw, setting the other creatures free. They all screamed as they scurried away from the other ocelot guarding the tree. They all fell to their deaths as the other ocelot knocked them off the high tree. A newborn stayed behind with his mother.

"Mommy!" the young one screamed.

"It's okay, darling," the female said between tears.

"Oh, how touching," Oxalamar said sarcastically. He then put a piece of bark in front of the entrance to the tree, letting just enough light into the tree but sealing it tight enough so that the tiny creatures wouldn't escape. He took the creature that he killed and started to eat it in front of them. The prisoners squinted as blood squirted at their faces.

"Mommy," repeated the newborn.

Oxalamar looked at the newborn and breathed on him.

The female squinted from the stench of her dead group member. "You're cruel!" the female screamed at him.

"I see you don't know who I am, do you? I am the king of the ocelots. I will soon be the king of the forest of rain!" he said proudly.

A sudden knock came from the door. "Come in," Oxalamar said. The bark that Oxalamar had put at the entrance got pushed down, but the creatures did not dare to move.

"We have Panthra." The two ocelots bowed and walked away.

"I understand you need my services," Panthra stated. Her black pelt echoed like death in the night. "You have death surrounding you. I like that." Panthra nodded. "What exactly would you like me to do?" she asked, looking at the creatures with bright eyes.

"I need you to be my guard. I also have a quest for you. If you do it, I will give you the north side of the forest of rain to rule."

Panthra nodded darkly. "What will be the deed you want me to perform?"

Oxalamar suddenly took his female prisoner and picked her up. He started to pet her. "I need you to kill two pesky tamarins that keep interfering with my plans. You may kill anyone else who is with them."

Panthra started to drool. "May I have those delicious creatures?"

Oxalamar nodded while passing the female to her. He quickly hit the newborn, sending him flying toward Panthra.

"It will be done," she said darkly.

Chapter 21

The First Attempt

Heraex's eyes were still full of tears the next day.

"It's okay, Heraex."

Heraex turned on him. "No, it's not! I'm going to die, and that's that!" Heraex then sat down on the branch.

Gold thought that it was best to not say anything and let Heraex deal with it on her own. He turned and looked at Cyndar. "Is that really what will happen?" he asked him with sadness in his voice.

Cyndar nodded slowly with regret. "I'm afraid so." Cyndar suddenly lifted his head up to the sky. "Something's wrong. Something's coming. We have to get inside the tree!" Cyndar exclaimed.

Gold was confused with Cyndar. What did he mean? A roar came from the trees not too far from them. "What was that?" Gold asked, surprised.

"That's what we should be running from!" Cyndar screamed as he started to climb fast up the tree to the opening of Heraex's home.

"Heraex, come on! Hurry!" Cyndar urged.

Heraex slowly got up from where she was sitting and climbed up the tree to where they were waiting.

"Heraex? Do you think we could go in your tree?" Gold asked.

Heraex nodded and led the way, emotionless. The creature then emerged from the ferns. A black, slick body became visible in the moonlight. Its white fangs were sharp and seemed to devour the whole forest. Blood dripped from them, indicating the beast must have already eaten. They all stayed very still.

"Heraex, don't move," Gold whispered.

The creature's ears twitched for a second then went back to normal. It started to drool on the ground. It started to drink the rainwater that fell as it scanned the tree with it eyes. The creature walked up closer to the tree that the three animals were on. Gold then suddenly felt something under his foot. The small branch that he was putting his weight on was about to break off. Before he could take his weight off it, it cracked.

The large creature then looked up to the three of them. "There you are. It took a while to find you," it said with a dark smirk.

Gold could easily tell that the creature was in league with Oxalamar.

"In case you were wondering, my name is Panthra. I do anything other people tell me to do in return for money or power."

Gold thought that this was a good time to make a quick jump since Panthra was too busy boasting.

"I wouldn't do that if I were you," she directed at Gold.

Gold, scared, hurried back to the same spot he was on.

"That's better. But do you know what the problem is? I have been wasting my time talking to you when I should have killed you by now." Her last words turned into battle cries as she pounced up the tree toward them.

"Awadien Calamak!" Cyndar shouted at Panthra.

She unexpectedly stopped in her tracks when a fireball shot at her. The spinning ball of flames left trails of sparks behind it as it flew toward the creature. The fireball hit her, sending her falling off the tree but not killing her. She rolled on the ground, making the fire die out. Gold let out a gasp of surprise at Cyndar.

"I'll explain later, but now we have to run!" They both scurried up the tree bark and on the branch leading into Heraex's home. Memory flashed back at Gold. He remembered how Heraex had saved him from the fall and how she saved him from the water filling up her tree.

"Don't waste any time! Hurry and get into the tree before she comes back!"

A sudden weight started to shake the branch they were on. "I think it would be hard to lose me," Panthra said in a sinister way.

"Can't you do another one of those fireballs, Cyndar?" Gold asked at the last minute while they were all walking backward, away from Panthra.

"No. That one weakened me. I can't do it until I regain my strength," he said, out of breath.

Gold kept walking backward until he hit a bump. He looked behind him. It was the tree entrance! He looked down in the tree and saw a frightening sight. The tree was still flooded with water! Other monkeys still walked around as if the water was nothing but air. *Just like Heraex.* He thought. Panthra came closer to them. Her jaws opened, and she came nearer to them.

"Heraex! Do you still have that crystal?"

Heraex nodded. "It's in the bag!"

Gold looked at her and blinked. "Well, get it!" he exclaimed.

She flipped the bag over her head and grabbed the crystal from the bottom of the bag. As Panthra came closer with her jaws open, Heraex put the crystal in the creature's mouth. "Where do I send her?" she asked impatiently.

"I don't know! Anywhere!" Cyndar yelled back.

Gold's ears began to sting because Cyndar screamed so loud.

"Send Panthra to the bottom of the volcano!" Heraex screamed, thinking fast.

The black pelt of the creature began to shine. Her teeth began to disappear with an outlined blue color. Her amber eyes shone, then her pupils disappeared into thin air. This process continued throughout her whole body until she disappeared altogether.

Sighs of relief came from all three of the animals. Gold turned to Cyndar. "So, do you mind telling us how you knew how to do that?" Gold questioned.

Chapter 22

Cyndar's Story

"It all started like this," Cyndar began to explain. "I was born along with three other coatis. There was a prophecy that said when four coatis are born at midnight, they will be the guardians of the elements. Each of us was born with a certain symbol that represented our powers."

Cyndar stopped and showed Gold and Heraex his arm. It had a symbol on it that kind of looked like a burning flame. "I was born with the fire symbol. The prophecy had named me Cyndar, so I had to take that name. I had one brother and two sisters. My brother's name was Aqua. He was the guardian of water. Aqua could also do so many amazing things like make it rain and throw water at someone out of thin air. He even got into freezing, but that same ocelot killed him, along with my two sisters. One of my sisters was Airial. She could control air and wind while my other sister, Terra, could control earth and nature. As you can see, I can control fire. I can make fireballs appear out of the heat of the air, and I can do many more things too.

"When we got older, we learned how to control our powers with the help of our mentor, Metalic. He wasn't a guardian of elements, but he could control types of matter. He taught us how to use our powers and help other animals with them. He was a good creature until Oxalamar killed him. After one guardian is killed, his or her power goes into a defense mode and is locked inside an orb. When the orb opens, the power goes to the next nearest guardian. Once all of the guardians die, their powers then go to others, and they become guardians. Once they become guardians, another mentor is called to help them with their powers. Not only did Metalic die, so did my three siblings."

Gold had a puzzled look on his face. "But why didn't you get their powers?"

Cyndar looked up at him. "Oxalamar must have been curious about the orbs, so he took them. None of them has broken yet. If they did, I would have the other powers of the elements. So like I was saying, when my siblings died, I was all on my own. I had no one else to help me protect the other creatures of the forest of rain. But you, there's something about you, Gold."

Gold jumped back in surprise. "What do you mean there's something about me?"

Cyndar nodded. "I think that you might be a guardian too."

Heraex blinked, but she didn't seem that surprised.

"A guardian of what?" Gold said with a tint of disbelief.

"Time," Heraex suddenly said with no expression.

"Exactly! You're the guardian of time," he told Gold.

"I don't get it though. Didn't you say that there were only four guardians—fire, water, air, and earth?"

Heraex looked at Gold and opened her mouth, "Sometimes, when the earth is in a very bad state, a new guardian appears. I think that you might be the most important one."

Gold was speechless. He couldn't believe he was a guardian just like Cyndar. "But I can only go to the past and the future in my dreams."

Cyndar looked shocked. "You can? That's perfect! You are already learning how to use your powers. Soon you will be able to do many more things with time. But beware, once you do them, you get extremely tired afterward."

Gold nodded in understanding. "Could you show me what you can do?"

Cyndar then put his paw up. A sudden spark flickered in the air and went wherever Cyndar moved his paw. It then burst into flames and twirled into a swirling, fiery tornado. As soon as Cyndar placed his paw on the bark, the bright red fire swirled back into his paw where it came out of, and the brightness disappeared into the night of the forest. Rain poured and bounced off the bark and to the river below them. Gold looked down at the river and started to get concerned.

"Now you try," said Cyndar.

Gold seemed to sweat. "But I'm not tired right now."

Cyndar let out a little bit of a chuckle. "You don't need to go to sleep. That's just an easier way of accessing your powers. Okay. Concentrate really hard on your power, time. Something might happen."

Gold thought about it a little bit and then gave in to Cyndar's idea. He concentrated on his power. He repeated the word *time* over and over in his head.

He heard Heraex's breathing starting to fade until it stopped. The same thing happened to Cyndar's a few seconds later. He opened his eyes and gasped in astonishment. Heraex and Cyndar were frozen in time! The rain even stopped, and the air seemed to stand still. He inspected Heraex and Cyndar to see if they were making a joke, but they wouldn't move or breathe. He touched the frozen rain. It glittered as it retained its shape after Gold put his nail through the liquid. He thought it was amazing. He imagined all of the things he could do with it.

Within twenty seconds, the rain began to fall again. All the sounds of different animals and the raindrops began to fill his ears again.

Heraex's breathing began to pick up, and she gasped in amazement. "But weren't you just over there?" Heraex asked as she pointed a tail-length away from where he was standing now.

"Uh, yeah," he said tiredly.

"You did it, Gold!" Cyndar exclaimed.

"Yeah." Gold's voice trailed off as he hit the tree branch with a loud bump. He closed his eyes and fell asleep from nausea.

Chapter 23

Attack

Gold opened his eyes under the tree canopy.

"Orange?" Heraex asked him.

Gold nodded, but he found himself weakened after moving.

"That took a lot out of you," Cyndar said as he walked out of a mass of leaves.

"Yeah. It did," Gold said in a whispery voice.

"What did you do, anyway?" Cyndar questioned.

Gold waited a while after he took his first bite of the orange Heraex had given him. After gaining enough strength, he sat up, looked toward Cyndar's direction, and replied, "I think I froze time."

An excited look washed upon Cyndar's face. The whites around his eyes seemed to glow with happiness. "Of course! Freezing time. How come I never thought of that? Here's the thing though, when you use a lot of your power, your energy gets drained until you master that ability. I remember when I tried to make a fireball for the first time. I was asleep for days."

An idea suddenly shook Gold. *How long was he asleep?* "How long was I asleep?" he asked demandingly.

"About four days. Why?" Cyndar asked.

Were they crazy? If he was asleep for four days, then Oxalamar could attack at any moment. The boost of adrenaline made Gold jump up to his feet.

"We have to get ready!" Gold announced. "Oxalamar and his gang of ocelots could be here any minute!" Gold shouted in panic. He had a feeling that Cyndar and Heraex hadn't thought about that yet until he told them.

"Well, we must get ready. The guardian of time, the guardian of fire, and an invincible tamarin shouldn't have that much of a hard time fighting, but still, we must be prepared for whatever those creatures throw at us."

Once Cyndar's speech ended, Gold got a sudden idea. "We could train!" Gold shouted.

The expression on Cyndar's face indicated that he thought this was a good idea. "Okay, let's train."

The leaves blew back and forth, still attached to their stems, while Gold walked quietly in between them. He then saw Cyndar confronting Heraex.

"Mlak Salaicta!" Cyndar shouted. A fireball then appeared from inside Cyndar's mouth. When he leaned forward and opened his mouth even wider, the fireball then shot out from his mouth and toward Heraex!

Gold closed his eyes and concentrated on time. He opened his eyes again once the sounds stopped and saw an amazing sight. He could see a scared expression on Heraex's face while the fireball blazed in front of her. He could see some hairs starting to blacken from the hot ball of fire. He decided he would move Heraex. After all, it would save her the trouble of healing. If he wanted to do this, he had to do this fast. The other time he froze time, it only lasted for twenty seconds, and ten had already passed.

Gold quickly jumped and took Heraex down with him as time resumed. The fireball skimmed the hair on their backs.

"Good job," Cyndar stated directly at Gold.

"Thanks," he said as Heraex pushed him off with her hind legs.

"Don't let anything distract you in battle," Cyndar told him.

Heraex lunged for Gold, her teeth showing. Gold then closed his eyes and thought about time once again. Heraex then stopped in midair, giving him a chance to move. He rushed behind her. Time began again after five seconds, and Heraex tumbled to the ground face first.

Gold jumped on her and dug his claws into her flesh. The blood evaporated off Gold's claws and got sucked into the wound the same way it came out. The skin stitched back together, and Heraex opened her eyes. Her body sat up, and she shoved Gold off.

"Malkarria Shaatashia!" a sudden voice chanted.

It suddenly began to get hotter as flames encircled them. They began to twirl around them in a sort of a twister of fire. He watched Heraex jump through the flames and to the other side where no fire flickered. Gold found himself in a death-or-life situation. He was too weak to stop time again, and he couldn't walk through the flames as Heraex did.

An idea suddenly struck him. He looked up and saw an opening from the flames. He had never tried it before, but he had to try hard. He bent down really low. After he bent as low as he could go, he sprang up from the floor and jumped through the opening. As he sprang up from the flames, he could see how big the twirling flames were.

"Reverse!" Cyndar shouted after he saw Gold jumped out of the fire twister. The flames dispersed and disappeared a few seconds after, leaving Gold landing back on his stomach.

"Great job!" Cyndar chuckled. "You did exactly as I wanted you to do—you relied on your physical strength more than your powers."

Heraex walked up to Gold. "Good match. I think you are going to be more than great when battling the ocelot," she said with a smile.

Gold felt more wanted than ever at this moment. He looked over at Cyndar. He had a strange look on his face. He looked scared and disturbed both at the same time.

"Oh, no," Cyndar said, worry washing through his voice.

"What?" Heraex asked him.

"They are coming. Brace yourselves," he said with no expression.

Gold got into a fighting stance, Heraex at his side. Cyndar got ready as though he was about to say something and set the whole tree on fire. A series of growls sounded from the distance of the trees. They were mottled with evil and dread. As the growling got closer, Gold knew the battle was near. Without warning, two ocelots sprang out of the leaves and went straight for Cyndar.

"Hakalima Bashaata!" Cyndar screamed. Cyndar then spun around and shot his tail at one of the ocelots. Fire appeared from the tip of his tail and shot at the ocelot. Its fur burst into flames, leaving the ocelot uncoordinated. It then fell off the branch and into the water a few feet below them. The water steamed as the dead corpse floated away down the river.

After the first ocelot fell, Heraex jumped on the other ocelot and dug her claws into its thick skin. Blood leaked from the wound as Heraex did a back flip off him and onto the bark in front of Gold. The ocelot fell from the branch and, like the other one, fell into the water and floated away.

Blood dripped from the branches as three more ocelots jumped from the leaves. Then, Oxalamar appeared. His gray body seemed to darken the whole tree.

"We can't do it. There are too many of them!" Heraex exclaimed.

Oxalamar laughed in the darkness. "Of course you can't beat me. I'm the ruler of the forest of rain. I'm surprised how you managed to beat my two guards though. No problem, my last three will easily kill you all." He laughed an evil laugh while the three ocelots sprang for the three animals.

As one of the ocelots sprang for him, Gold closed his eyes and thought of freezing time. This time when he opened his eyes, the ocelot did not stop in the air. It was going in slow motion, getting closer and closer to his throat each second. At least it gave him time to think about what he was going to do next. He did the same thing he did to Heraex. He rushed to the back of the ocelot and waited until real time resumed instead of slow motion. The ocelot banged his head against the branch and slipped off the wet bark. Gold could hear him roaring as the current swept him away farther from the tree. Gold then looked beside him as one of the ocelots retreated from Heraex and went to the side of Oxalamar. He heard the ocelot whisper something to its leader, and Oxalamar walked closer to Gold.

"So you're pretty powerful. I should have known," Oxalamar told him. Oxalamar then lifted his paw, and three shiny orbs followed. Three colors shined from them as they floated in the air. Gold suddenly remembered that those were the powers of the fallen guardians. Gold had to break them! Gold quickly flew for one of the orbs and broke a blue one. Water busted from the orb and went toward Cyndar. The water went into Cyndar's eyes and mouth. Gold heard a sudden scream of hurt. It was from Cyndar.

After all of the water washed throughout his body, Cyndar smiled. He then stood up on his two back legs and put up his two paws. Water then flowed through his hands and toward the ocelot that was attacking him. The jets of water made the ocelot fly backward into another tree. It then fell into the water like all of the others.

"Uh-oh, I don't think so," Oxalamar whispered to Gold. "You're not getting these ones," he said with a smile.

Before Gold could do anything, Oxalamar threw the two other orbs into the river, making them float away.

"No!" Gold screamed. Before Gold could jump after them, one of the guards jumped on him, pinning him down on a branch. "Heraex! Help!" Gold's voice was hardly anything but a whisper because one of the ocelot's paws was against his voice box. Gold then remembered something. "Wait!" Gold screamed when he saw Heraex rushing for the ocelot. She stopped in confusion. "We need him for the curse," Gold whispered to her. Understanding washed over her face. This was it.

Chapter 24

Farewell

The air pressing on Gold's throat made it harder to breath. It was time; he had to do it now. Using all of his strength, he sprang up, making the ocelot go flat on Heraex's tree. "Go, Cyndar!" Gold yelled at him.

Cyndar then let out a chant and threw a bright red fireball at the ocelot, throwing it against the tree. Blood gushed out of the ocelot, smearing the tree.

Gold looked back at Oxalamar and smiled. "Not so tough now, huh?" he said with a tint of sarcasm. He saw Oxalamar weaken and trembled on his feet. The other ocelot finally died on the tree, its blood staining it.

"Heraex?" a voice yelled out from the entrance of the tree.

"Mom!" Heraex screamed back. Heraex trembled as she walked to her mother. The rain drenched her mother's black hair as she walked out of the entrance. The curse was being broken! Everything was finally ending. A hint of sadness peeked through Gold's eyes. Tears poured down his face as he watched Heraex getting weaker by the second.

"Heraex," he whispered.

Cyndar ran up to him. "The tree's glowing!"

Gold glanced at the tree and the blood on the tree started to glow. The rain got lighter. He put his hand on the glowing parts of the tree, and a sudden sucking noise came from behind him. He looked and saw a porthole like the one that past Gold got sucked into a few weeks ago. Gold watched as Heraex and her mother walked up to him.

A roar came from behind them. Suddenly, a monster with huge teeth and tiny arms walked out of the porthole. Its large tail swooped from side to side as it ran away into the forest.

"What was that?" Gold asked, surprised by the appearance of the beast.

"The porthole opened for too long! Other creatures from different times are running out!" Cyndar screamed.

A big thump stopped their conversation. Gold looked behind him and saw a huge slothlike creature. It wasn't as big as the sloth they rescued from the shadow creatures earlier; it was about fifty times bigger!

Gold watched as it slowly walked through the forest. He watched in amazement as two large birds with purple and blue feathers walked out of the porthole and ran out of sight. More animals ran out or flew from the porthole and scattered in all directions. His pupils grew as he locked eyes with Cyndar. He was as speechless as he was.

"Goodbye," came a soft voice from Heraex.

Gold watched in sadness, and her feet started to turn to dust and ash. "It won't be long until I'm gone," she said as the dust started to engulf her knees.

"Bye, Heraex, you are the best friend I've ever had. Thank you for everything," he said between tears.

"You're welcome, Gold," she said with a smile. She looked down and saw her stomach turn to ash and dust. "You have to go after those creatures," she told him. "Remember, you're the key." Her last few words were whispers as her whole body turned to dust and ash and flew into the porthole.

"Heraex! No!" he said as he let tears pour out. He looked over at Oxalamar.

"My plans are ruined! Thanks to you!" Oxalamar shouted as his face turned to dust along with his body, and he got sucked into the porthole.

Another animal walked out of the porthole and ran for cover. Gold couldn't identify this animal though. It ran away too fast. None of this mattered anymore. Heraex was gone. He then remembered her last words: "Remember, you're the key." This last statement created confidence in Gold. He then stood up and walked past the ashes that were once Heraex's mother. It then got sucked into the porthole.

He watched, entranced that it was once Heraex's mother, and saw ash and dust getting sucked out of the tree entrance and poured into the porthole. He looked up at the sky and saw the clouds finally clear, and the rain stopped pounding on the leaves and the bark. The sunrays then illuminated the trees, leaving Gold's eyes blinded for a few seconds. After the blindness wore off, he looked up to the top of the tree. It was turning into dust too, from top to bottom.

"Cyndar, come on!" he screamed at him as they ran to another tree. Cyndar followed him, and they both watched Heraex's tree turn to dust and got sucked into the porthole.

A sudden loud bang came from the porthole. It then closed with a big spark of light and disappeared into thin air. The sunny day was then quiet. The noises of animals filled the skies as Gold dropped on the bark. It was over! The curse was broken. He watched the sunrays glitter in the light. He looked down into the river.

"I could have gotten those power orbs," he told Cyndar as he let one last tear fall down his cheek. Gold then looked above him, to the forest of rain's canopy. He then saw something poking out of the tree. He jumped up and grabbed it. It was Heraex's bag—the one they had used to carry all of their stuff in. He looked at the bag for about ten minutes, then he heard something from the river.

"Gold?" a voice called from below. It was that river beast!

"River beast!" he screamed with joy.

"Wow! You've gotten bigger, haven't you?" the river beast asked in happiness.

"Yeah," he said between tears once again.

"Are these yours?" the river beast asked as he flipped and sent two shiny orbs toward Gold.

"Yes, they are! Thank you so much, river beast!"

The river beast then nodded and swam off, flipping in the distance.

Gold looked down at the shining orbs. Cyndar smiled and put them into Heraex's bag.

"I never thought I could pull all of this off—fighting off howlers, avoiding shadow creatures, surviving eruptions," Gold said.

Cyndar looked at him and chuckled with his old crackling voice. After all, this was only the beginning.

Breinigsville, PA USA
22 June 2010
240320BV00001B/68/P